Viviane Moore was born
photographer at 19, she later became a freelance writer, and has contributed to various European magazines. Her great knowledge of France in the Middle Ages has led her to write quite a number of detective novels, all set in the twelfth century.

By the same author

A Black Romance

BLUE BLOOD

VIVIANE MOORE

Translated by
Rory Mulholland

An Orion paperback

First published in Great Britain in 2000
By Victor Gollancz
This paperback edition published in 2001
by Orion Books Ltd,
Orion House, 5 Upper St Martin's Lane,
London WC2H 9EA

A CIP catalogue record for this book is available from the British Library.

ISBN 0 57540 319 5

Printed and bound in Great Britain by
Clays Ltd, St Ives plc

Prologue

I killed her.

I saw her writhe in the flames. I heard her scream as she died.

And since . . . Every night she comes to haunt me, disfigured by fire, blackened and bloody.

I have wanted to pluck out my eyes, cut off my hands, smash my body, lay waste to my soul . . . And death has rejected me.

Neither God nor the Devil want me . . . Not yet.

Every night her life bleeds on the stake which I have lit.

God, deliver me! Cut through the flesh that constricts me. Give me more than death! Give me eternal oblivion!

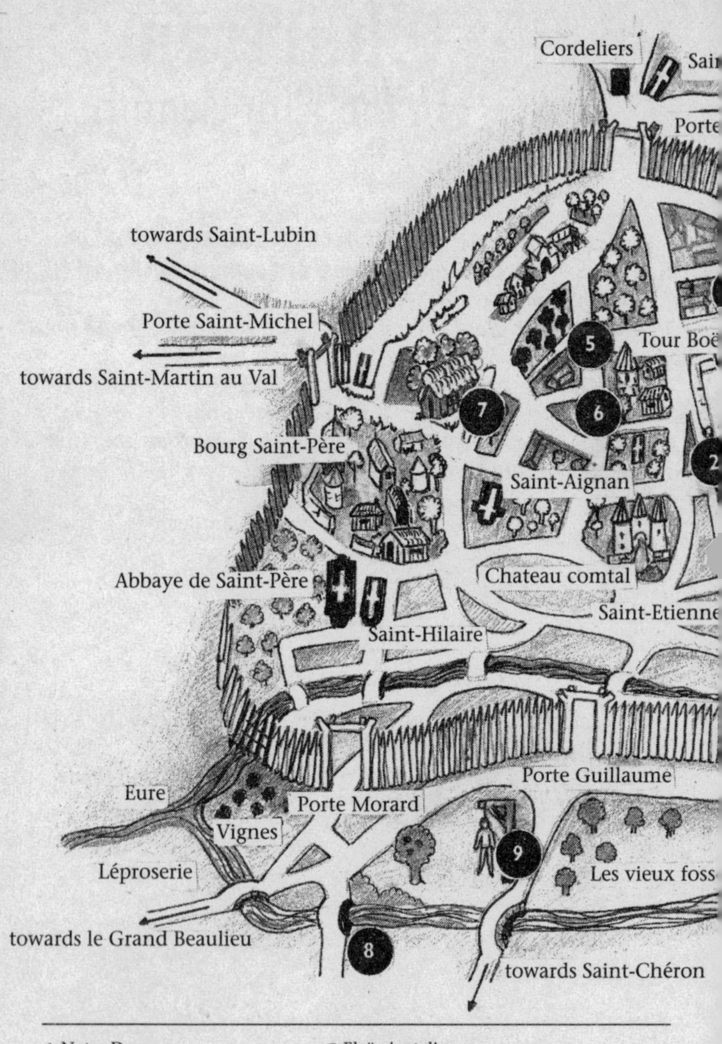

1 Notre Dame
2 The Rovin Vignon
3 Audouard's house
4 Ausanne's house
5 Mallon the goldsmith's
6 Eloïse's atelier
7 The Coeur Couronné
8 The old woman of the river's shack
9 The gallows

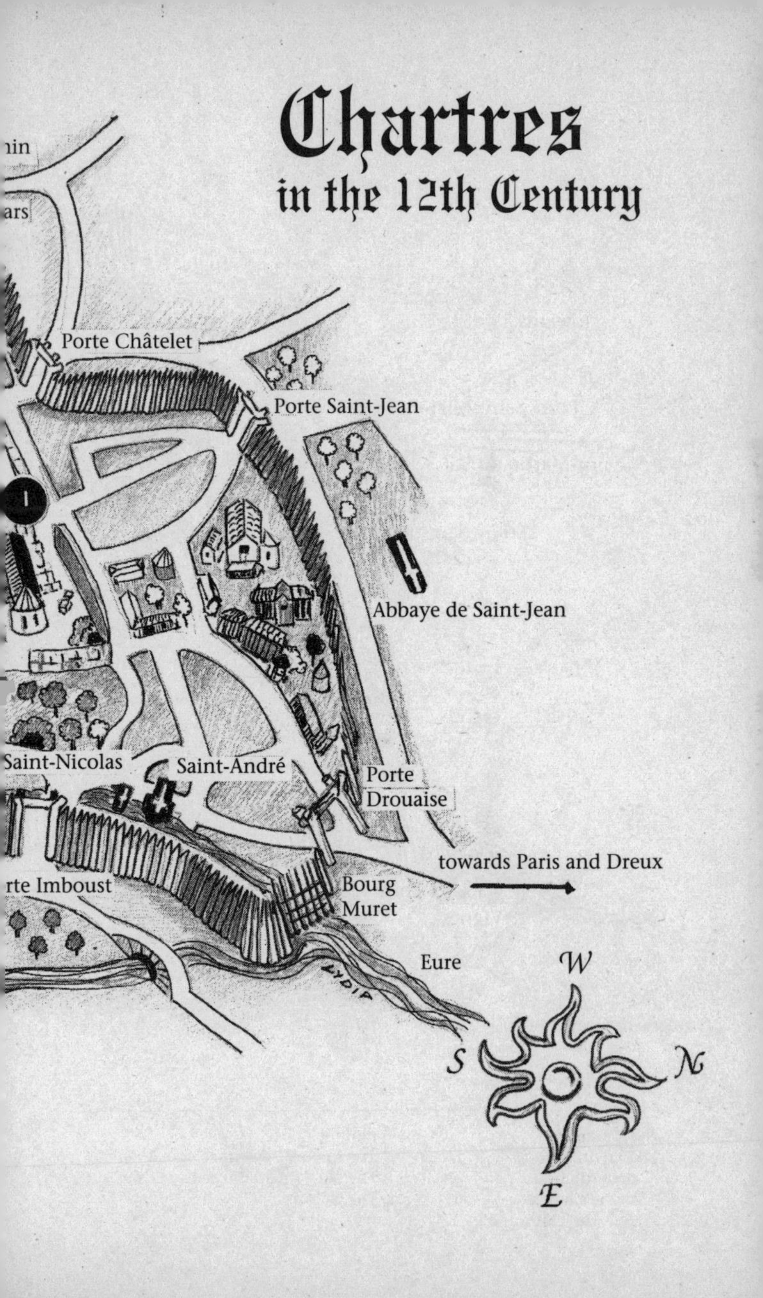
Chartres
in the 12th Century
Porte Châtelet
Porte Saint-Jean
Abbaye de Saint-Jean
Saint-Nicolas
Saint-André
Porte
Drouaise
towards Paris and Dreux
Bourg
Muret
Eure
LYDIA
W
S
N
E

PART ONE

Thou shalt not be afraid for the terror by
night, nor for the arrow that flieth by
day,
Nor for the pestilence that walketh in
darkness, nor for the destruction that
wasteth at noonday.

Psalms 91, 5–6

1

In the month of May in the year 1145, the moon was as red and fleeting as a vixen. The torches that flickered in the stone recesses of montjoys were the only lights to be seen in the streets of Chartres.

The sound of marching feet echoed across the cobbled stones of Rue Saint-Père. Men-at-arms, torchlight shimmering on their coats of mail, were on their way back to their quarters at the end of their patrol. They had made a detour down by the river during which they found only a few prowling drunkards, and were now heading in the direction of the Palais Comtal, the seat of regional power, and the cathedral of Notre Dame.

Two figures scurried to hide in the darkness of a stone porch. The soldiers hurried by, keen to warm themselves at the hearth before retiring to their straw mattresses. The dancing glow of their torches receded and silence reigned once more. Large clouds swept across the sky and threw their shadows across the walls of the upper town.

Suddenly it began to rain, and streams of mud were soon pouring down the sloping streets. The two figures emerged cautiously from their bolt-hole.

'By God, but he's heavy!' cursed one of them, a man, shifting the hessian sack on his back with a thrust of the shoulder.

'For pity's sake, be quiet and get a move on!' a woman's voice beseeched him. 'Do you want the Provost's men to catch us?'

The long, hooded, brown capes the couple wore lent them a monastic air. They advanced carefully, passing through lane after lane until they arrived in a gloomy little square. On their left was a narrow alleyway between two rows of houses. The passage, sombre and stinking of urine, led them straight to an old, disused postern which opened onto the river Eure. They pushed it open and stood silently for a moment on the step. It was so dark they could barely make out the muddy footpath at their feet that led off into the blackness.

The russet moon re-emerged from behind the clouds and the couple headed off down the track. They descended step by step, their muscles tense, gripping the bushes to stop themselves from slipping. A bird suddenly flew up in front of them, its long wings brushing the earth. The woman stifled a cry.

At the end of the footpath they found a jetty, made of worm-eaten wood, lapped by the choppy waters of the Eure. With a sigh of relief, the man let his burden slip down onto the ground.

He opened the bag and a body began to slide out: first came the hanging head, the glazed eyes, the grey hair darkened with blood, then the pale torso, and finally the legs with their bony knees. The woman silently opened a leather satchel and took out some clothes and a pair of old boots which she placed in a pile on the steps.

'When they find him they'll think it was an accident. They'll think the old man wanted to go for a swim in the nice warm weather, but that his strength abandoned him,' she murmured, as though to herself.

She appeared to consider the matter a moment longer, and then, without any apparent concern for the rain, threw back her hood. She bent over the cadaver. A strange smile played upon her lips and in her hand glinted a short, sharp blade. She ran its point over the dead man's face before swiftly cutting through the rope that tied his hands and feet.

'You stupid fool!' she hissed, her eyes half-closed as if in reverie. 'None of this would have happened if you'd done my bidding.'

'Hurry, let's throw him into the water!' the man growled. 'We cannot linger here. We could be spotted by a patrol or some reveller. Come on! Hup!'

Gripping the body under the armpits as though it were a toy, he flung it into the river before the woman had time to move. The black water took possession of the corpse, which turned over and floated away like a dead fish buoyed by the current.

Anger darkened the woman's face. She got up and drew closer to her accomplice. She cut a striking and beautiful figure, her fingers clenching the handle of her dagger, the rain streaming down over her long braided hair, over her eyebrows and onto her face.

Her companion seemed unconcerned by the weapon she brandished. He moved towards her until their bodies touched. The woman was tense, her lips half-open. She let the blade slip from her fingers.

The man embraced her, almost lifting her off the ground, and forced his mouth upon hers. She responded by biting him and making him bleed. He tightened his embrace and their bodies fused, indifferent to the world around them.

Then he brusquely pulled away. The young woman trembled, her eyes blank and her lips white. She did not react when he pulled up her hood and buttoned her cape. He bent down and pocketed the dagger lying in the wet grass, threw the severed ropes into the darkness and hid the sack among some thick mulberry bushes.

Surveying the scene one last time, he slipped his arm around his companion's slim waist and the pair began climbing back towards the upper town. As they walked up the steps, the man took care that the comely form at his side did not stumble or fall.

2

A solitary figure, dressed in a black tunic and dark breeches, stood on the wooden scaffolding of one of the towers of Notre Dame cathedral. His hand gripping a rail, he leaned towards the mist-shrouded town below him. The rain had stopped. A sparrowhawk spiralled in the sky. The man, his face hidden by a hood, seemed tense, as though awaiting a signal that only he would recognise.

The morning Angelus bell rang out. Its vibrations shook the sanctuary and seemed to call forth the sounds of the town: the morning cries, the creaking of wheels on the cobbles, the whinnying of horses, the banter of men on their way to work. Guided by the calls of their shepherd, a flock of sheep struggled up the hill towards Place des Halles. It was as though the town had suddenly, brutally almost, come to life. The mist slowly broke up to make way for a sun that was already warm.

Merchants' canopies were creakily erected. Men and women swarmed over the cobblestones of Chartres, setting up trestle tables in front of the houses. The stalls on Rue au Lin, Rue de la Pelleterie, Rue du Marché au Blé, and Rue au Vin were soon covered in goods: vegetables, fruit, spices from the Orient, aromatic herbs, fish, meat, fabrics, leather, gold- and silverware.

The area by the river, below the upper town, was also coming alive. This was where wool and yarn were treated. Mill workers were arriving at their ateliers to begin their day's labour. Some were already beating the untreated wool to clean it, others carded it with thistles.

Robust matrons loaded the skeins of wool thus prepared onto wicker baskets which they would then carry on their backs, huffing and puffing, to the weavers in the upper town.

Nearby, master dyers watched over their vats. Each specialised in a different colour. Wool, when they treated it with madder, emerged a very pure red. Fabrics dipped in woad would, if the dyer had kept a very close eye on his vat, turn out a celestial blue, the colour of the immortal soul. And weld resulted in a yellow as bright as the sun.

A portly man, a dyer's assistant by trade, stood weighing ash. He needed precise measurements to produce the alum that enabled fabric to retain dye after washing.

A little further along, near Porte Guillaume, some men were hanging sheets on metal hooks before setting in motion a system of pulleys that served to stretch the cloth for bleaching in the sun. Mules, guided by young boys, then ferried the sheets to Bourg Saint-Père.

Through the gates of the town streamed masons, carpenters, stonecutters, glassworkers, all heading towards the site where the great cathedral of Notre Dame was being built. Chartres had been ravaged by a fire on a cursed September day in 1134, and for the past ten years the community had been busily rebuilding their town.

Songs and laughter rang out through the air. Pilgrims, come to adore the Veil of the Blessed Virgin, congregated near the crypt for the first office of the day.

Schoolchildren, recognisable by their tunics of grey cloth, quickened their step, already late for their first lessons. A tiny child scurried after his mother, a sturdy washerwoman, her hips bearing a basket of dirty laundry.

The man in black seemed to hesitate as he stood on his lofty perch. His face darkened at the sight of the workers clambering up the wooden ladders of the cathedral. He gathered up a bag filled with well-worn tools, turned and moved off, like an uncertain tightrope walker, towards an unfinished sculpture of a mythical animal, half-man, half-bird.

3

The knight sat impassive and erect as his mount advanced at a jog-trot. The slanting arrows of the spring sun that pierced the treetops played on this enigmatic figure barded in leather and metal.

In a few weeks, if the fine weather held, the foliage would be much thicker and the great forest would again become a dark jungle where imprudent travellers would lose their way. Yet the forest was thinning with each new day. The tracks made by the ever greater numbers of men and horses were becoming wider. Woodcutters' camps, hermitages and forges were springing up. Carpenters from the fortified towns or from the cathedrals now had to go east towards the Kingdom of Burgundy to find a steady supply of hardwood trees.

'If it continues like this,' the knight said to himself, smiling, 'even the magic Brocéliande that held captive Artus le Gallois's men will soon be no more than a legend!'

Galeran de Lesneven had not seen a living soul since his dawn departure from the château of Gallardon. He rode in silence, always on the alert, always ready for the unexpected. This sense of danger was second nature to him now, an old habit but one that did not prevent him from drifting off into reverie as he rode along on Quolibet, his tranquil seven-year-old gelding.

The beast's gait was steady, even a little lumbering. But at the approach of battle Galeran would feel him quiver beneath him. The furious cries of the combatants, the clash of arms, the blaring of the horns and trumpets of war excited him as much as they did his master. He would become tense, his ears pricked up, his nostrils flaring, and suddenly launch himself into combat as others would into water. His movements would then become gracious, he would weave his way through the mêlée, instinctively anticipating the blows of adversaries and manoeuvring to facilitate those his rider dealt out.

After the exhaustion of combat, well fed, rubbed down and

his wounds duly treated, he would magically regain his placid bearing, a little like a sword that one puts back in its scabbard until the next time it needs to be drawn.

As is often the case, horse and man had many common characteristics. For was not the knight also torn between a profound desire for peace and a passion that led him towards danger, as though his most noble faculties could only be exercised at death's door, when body and soul were united?

He often asked himself by what stroke of political genius the Holy Church, in the name of Jerusalem, had in just a few lustra transformed the cruelty of the Crusades, which seemed to him an emanation of Armageddon, into a just cause.

'But, after all,' mused the knight, 'did not Christ love the good centurion as much as He did the prostitute?'

And had not he himself seen the Knights Templar charge furiously into battle against the Moors and the same evening, in the half-light of a church, sing Compline and become gentle and humble as lambs?

Galeran gently scratched Quolibet's neck.

'Yes,' he murmured to the horse, whose best fighting days were perhaps behind him, 'you are like a brother to me. We have travelled far together. You loved the clash of armour but now all you seek is the peace of the pasture. But, you know, man's Paradise is also a green pasture. At least, that's what they say!'

As though hypnotised by the vibrant light of the foliage, Galeran let himself slip again into thoughts of days gone by, and more specifically of events just one week before.

He had left Saint-Denis, crossed Paris and entered the forest of Yvelines in the direction of Chartres. On the way he had stopped for several days at the Abbey of Cernay to visit his friend Huon.

In 1118 the monks of Savigny cleared a plot of land in the forest to build a place of worship. The abbey they constructed was in the hollow of a small valley encircled by high hills. The wood, through which flowed a river, was populated with hundred-year-old oaks. The place had an almost magical charm. In the surrounding villages people said the monks used water from a ferruginous spring which had astonishing properties for treating the infirm.

'It is a solitude that lies deep within the forest and hidden by a procession of hills where God's servants live unseen,' were the words Bernard de Clairvaux used to describe his own abbey, and the description was also fitting for Huon's home.

Galeran recalled the light that played on the clear stone of the cloister, and thought of his friend's serene face. He could remember every word of their conversation.

'To love,' said the young monk, 'always means to leave behind the sad realities of this world. True love knows neither the banal nor that which, to others, may seem repugnant. I may clean the latrines or care for the bedridden, but if I love Christ these duties are gentle and agreeable to me.'

'So,' the knight replied with a laugh, 'our noble ladies are right to make servants of us, to test and to humilitate us.'

'You are correct, friend. It is thus that we serve Mary, our blessed mother who is Our Lady.'

They walked slowly along a paved path lined with well-tended holly bushes.

'The world is a troubling place, my friend,' Huon continued, 'because everything within it contains its own opposite. In evil there is good, and good is never sheltered from evil. But tell me, have you never been tempted to follow the example of Hugues de Payns or Geoffroy de Saint-Omer and join the Knight Templar? To take the three monastic vows along with the promise to serve Christ with your weapons?

The young knight smiled.

'Poor I am, but chaste and obedient – that would be too much to ask of a Breton knight so enamoured of liberty!'

Huon laughed, and considered the fine figure his friend cut.

The two men had met five years earlier on the road to Cernay. The young oblate had been attacked by a group of vagabonds. His monk's habit had not stopped the scoundrels from giving him a hiding, and the poor unfortunate owed his salvation to the knight who stepped in to help him. A firm friendship had developed between the two men, who in taste and temperament were so very different.

At the age of seven, Huon's family had given him to God.

Raised by monks, the only horizons he had ever known were the walls of monasteries. A small man with a moon-like face and forget-me-not eyes, he was all gentleness and serenity, as though filled with a strange inner clarity.

Galeran, for his part, liked to say he came from the end of the world. He was born into Breton family from the minor nobility, a family ruined by the First Crusade. He was tall, his black hair cropped, and he had a deep scar across his forehead. He had a lived-in face that was both gentle and devoid of complacency.

'You should rid yourself of the cares of this world, my friend,' insisted Huon. 'If you only knew how light it makes you feel!'

'And how should I do that? Neither a settled life in the town nor that of a recluse appeals to me. So all that is left is to wander the roads to find out about the world. The Orient interests me now, more than great deeds of war. We have much to learn from these Moors that we call heretics. They are more passionate than us about medicine, astronomy, and a host of other things. They are men of great learning.'

'Ah, learning! Do you believe, friend, that one must journey to acquire knowledge? We who remain behind our walls learn more than those who roam the highways. But, really, we two are not as different as you would have me believe. You are keener for books than for arms. You read Greek, Latin and Hebrew, and have mastered the liberal arts.'

'I deserve no credit for that, my friend.'

A jay flew up before them. The knight followed it for a moment with his eyes.

'My parents wanted me to have the education of a cleric,' he said. 'The Crusades left them impoverished, but still they provided me, from a very early age, with a learned master. It is thanks to them that I came to appreciate beauty, and it is thanks to my master that I learned how to seek out its meaning.'

Suddenly pensive, he fell silent. When he began to speak again, it was as though he were addressing himself:

'It was at the age of fourteen I took up arms. I have taken part in countless private wars and tournaments between lords.

I loved the applause and the gaze of women after the combat. I have been the death of many men, and death, many times, has nearly taken me.'

Galeran paused again.

'I must go now,' he said abruptly. 'I have to give Marcabru a shake. I'm sure the lazybones is still asleep.'

'Are you certain you wish to travel with him?' asked Huon.

'Oh, yes, despite his less than winning appearance and his swaggering, I have taken a shine to the man in my few days here in Vaux-de-Cernay. How long has he been lodging with you?'

'He arrived about ten days ago, and in such a pitiful state that it was a couple of days before we had him back on his feet again. But truth to tell, we are glad to see the back of him. He is not a good example for our novices. He spends his time singing bawdy songs and telling them stories about magic and satyrs and nymphs.'

'Forgive me, but it makes me laugh to think of that old devil teaching the meaning of life to a gang of bewildered novices. But, you know, what else can you expect from a troubadour whose bad temper and thieving has had him chased from every court in the land? You should keep a close eye on the abbey's treasure chest – Marcabru has a weakness for gold and silver, although they say he generally contents himself with borrowing the crockery!'

The knight smiled at the monk's discomfort.

'But fear not, Huon. I shall relieve you of him. We leave today for Gallardon, where we shall spend the night. But, by my faith, you shall see me again before long. This I swear to you, my friend.'

And upon these words Galeran took the monk's hands in his own and held them for a long moment before striding off to find Master Marcabru.

The young monk stood motionless for a while, his heart a little heavy at Galeran's departure. Huon was beginning to understand the knight's sudden moods and the strange mélange of introspection and action that informed his every gesture. He remembered the murder of Abbé Guillaume in Fontevrault, a seemingly insoluble mystery but one which the young knight had elucidated in a matter of days. Over the years his reputation had grown and he was often called upon to unravel enigmas that had stumped the secular or religious authorities.

Some eminent figures, such as Abbé Suger and Bernard de Clairvaux, had attempted to engage him, but without success. King Louis le Jeune also offered the knight a position as counsellor or ambassador at his court. But Galeran turned them all down, and managed to do so without upsetting any of them.

The only person who almost swayed him was Queen Aliénor of Acquitaine.

> Fair smiling eyes,
> Sweet and vermilion lips,
> Visage of rose and lily,
> Bosom of shimmering white . . .

The beautiful, and powerful, Aliénor was used to obedience from all quarters, including her own father and her spouse, King Louis. But Galeran had miraculously not only said no to this Queen of France, but had also made her his friend and loyal protector.

4

Marcabru did indeed turn out to be a good fellow traveller, and his mule got on well with the placid Quolibet.

Sleeping under the stars was second nature for two hardy men like Chevalier Galeran and his companion. Each night they chose a quiet spot to build their fire and boil some water in which to place their salted meat. After a few swigs from their bottle, they would launch into philosophical conversation interspersed with songs, picked out on the rebec, that told of the beauty and grace of noble ladies. And when they had had their fill of liquor and song they would piss on the fire to extinguish it, a task of which Master Marcabru was unduly fond. They then stretched out under their cloaks, in the shelter of the thick bushes, one eye open and their weapons within arm's length.

They soon arrived at the château of Gallardon. Galeran spent but one night there, for he wanted to press on. Marcabru decided to stay. The troubadour was low on supplies and needed to earn some money with his music. Moreover, he found the fresh young face of Sir Hervé de Gallardon's daughter much to his liking and worthy of a place in his repertory. He thought he might even honour her with a visit to her bed.

Galeran rose at dawn and was surprised to see the poet as he left the château. Despite getting sumptuously drunk the night before with Sir Hervé's men, Marcabru had risen early to take his leave of his companion.

'Fare thee well, Galeran! May the gods and the fairies shield you. Do not forget me. If the nymphs wish it, we shall meet again here or elsewhere, in this world or in the next.'

Marcabru stood and watched Galeran ride off. This morning he was grave in manner, his clothes dirty and his hair disorderly. Despite his celebrity, the man took little care over his appearance. All that mattered to him were the songs of Acquitaine and the money that his music and his romantic conquests enabled him to make off with.

5

Chartres was not far off, and the knight hoped he would arrive by Sext. He spurred his horse to a gallop on the forest path. The breeze was gentle and perfumed, his face was flushed and a smile was on his lips. The young man was as one with his steed. He bent forward over the beast's neck as it raced along the track, the gloss of sweat shining on its pelt.

Galeran recalled his last visit to Saint-Denis and the sombre story of the murder he had investigated. Now it was Thibaud IV, the Count of Blois, who had sent for him, no doubt to resolve some new mystery.

'In any case, it will give me an opportunity to call upon my old friend Audouard in Chartres and see the extraordinary cathedral he has told me so much about,' he thought.

Partridges flew up before him as he entered a clearing. Quolibet gave a sudden start that almost threw his rider and then stopped short, his nostrils flaring. A majestic stag sprang from a thicket in a crash of breaking branches. The animal stopped for an instant, stared at the knight with its brilliant eyes and regained the forest in three impressive bounds. Galeran quieted his horse, stroking its sweating neck, and then began to trot off, his head filled with this magical vision. Even in King Louis VII's hunting grounds he could not recall having seen such a magnificent creature.

'Ten-point stags are becoming almost as rare as fairies in the glades,' he mused. 'And, despite all Marcabru's promises, no pretty nymphs have come out from behind the thick bark of an oak tree to woo me.'

After several days riding through leafy shade, Galeran finally emerged from the forest. He took a bridle path snaking between two fields that rippled under the sun. Oats and millet formed a ring around the hill on which stood Chartres, separating the town from the forest. But the sight that most impressed Galeran was the immense fields of flax. Like a pale-blue sky that had been poured onto the earth, the crop's flowers followed the meanders of the river Eure to come to a halt at the foot of the hill.

Chartres majestically dominated the plain, topped by the ramparts of the upper town, Palais Comtal and the steeple of Notre Dame.

'Autricum,' murmured Galeran. 'City of the Carnutes. You reign over the plain of Beauce as our Queen, the lovely Aliénor, rules over her people.'

And the knight guided his steed towards the palisade.

Merchants, pilgrims and tumblers had joined the crowds of peasants and workers who thronged noisily around the gates of the town. Galeran passed through Bourg Muret and entered the town through Porte Drouaise. A tollgate at the entrance to the upper town slowed the passage of goods and people. Jostled by the crowd, the knight dismounted and, leading Quolibet by the bridle, made his way forward as best he could. The narrow passage into the upper town was further obstructed by carts bearing cut stone and vegetables and by men pushing barrows. Insults and broad jokes flew through the air. Men shook their fists at each other, and some verbal assaults even ended in fisticuffs.

Rue de la Corroierie was blocked by a convoy of tumbrils, so Galeran changed tack and wove his way towards Porte Imboust, taking Rue de la Petite Rivière along the Eure.

The river, much narrower at this point, gushed along the banks, working the blades of the mills. The place was of some beauty and the knight paused for a long moment to admire it. In a nearby meadow women were fulling sheets, their voluminous dresses hoisted up with belts. Their laughter and their song fused with the warm light of May.

A house on Rue du Soleil d'Or, easily recognisable by the beautiful sculptures on its corbelled façade, was home to a family of weavers whose most talented member, Éloïse, had seen only sixteen summers. Éloïse was known by all in the town of Chartres for her skill and her passion for weaving. She had been weaving since the age of six and her craft meant everything to her. It had taken such a grip that it was beginning to leave its mark on her frail, adolescent body. She had a slight stoop, her long, slender fingers were sinewy and her complexion was a pallid, milky-white.

Éloïse, her russet hair plaited and tied with a green ribbon, had gone to her atelier where she would resume work on a commission for Geoffroy de Lèves, the Bishop of Chartres. She put on her long white smock and looked closely at a charcoal crayon sketch on a small beechwood board. This board and the numbers she wrote thereon helped Éloïse to keep in her memory any figure, any detail of carpentry or of sculpture that interested her. Her examination complete, her mind returned to her craft, and she studied the work that lay before her.

Brightly coloured threads of linen, hemp and wool intertwined to produce a motif to which she alone possessed the key. But forms were already beginning to emerge in the work. It was possible to distinguish what would become a blue sky, leaves on a tree or a flower.

6

Galeran climbed up along Rue de la Perrée towards the Palais Comtal. After several hesitant detours along alleyways swarming with people, he arrived at the foot of the cathedral. As he looked up at the edifice he recalled the words of Abbé Suger: 'A magnificent work, flooded by a new and resplendent light.'

He observed, full of respect, the imposing mass of the sanctuary, the slender buttresses, the spires and the stone windows pierced by light, a vision of a celestial city born of the hand of man.

A red-haired boy of around twelve years of age perched on a pile of stones and watched Galeran. A short bow was slung over his shoulder and he wore a tunic, blue breeches and leather chausses. The head of a dead pigeon hung from the open top of his gamebag. His freckled face was serious, grave almost, as he scrutinised the knight's equipment.

Galeran wore a long purple tunic through whose vents could be seen a coat of fine chain mail. His brown cloak was flung back over his shoulders and fell down over his mount's hindquarters. His sword hung at his side in a deerskin baldric, and strapped to his back he carried a large red shield bearing a sable star. Another sword, a gamebag and a goatskin hanging from the pommel of his saddle completed the knight's outfit, his only fortune.

His head full of tales of the Crusades he had heard countless times, the boy imagined the knight was returning nom the Holy Land or from battles with the Almohads of Castille, the Moors who, it was said, had murdered Roland le Preux and chopped their Christian prisoners into tiny pieces.

It was his first visit to Chartres, but Galeran knew well the bustling atmosphere of towns where huge building projects were under way. Here, as at Saint-Denis, his first impression was of a place that was an astonishing mix of noisy disorder and extreme organisation. All the guilds were represented here, each worker knew exactly what his task was, and watching over everything was the foreman.

Intense activity reigned on the scaffolding that girded the building works. Stones were brought to the upper levels by wooden hoists known as gins. Masons made their mortar with the dust of the rock they had cut. Inclined planes enabled the workers, bearing heavy mortar boards, to reach the highest parts of the edifice. Stonecutters were busy at work on the façade and on the towers that soared above the town. The dull thump of carpenters' axes as they struck wood could be heard above the general din.

A little to one side stood a forge from which a spray of sparks flew up. Blacksmiths toiled there, repairing broken tools or preparing metal fittings for the doors or the high windows of the Royal Portal.

As Galeran observed the proceedings around him, he noticed that the little redhead was still watching him.

'Hey, boy, can you look after my horse for me? I have to go into the cathedral and horses are not very welcome there.'

'I can, Sir. And I'll give him a good rubbing down, for he looks hot and tired.'

'Give him some water, too. He has earned it.'

'You have come far, Sir?'

'A curious little fellow, are you not?'

'It is rare that I see a knight, and rarer still one with a shield and swords like your own. Whom do you seek in the cathedral?'

'Watch out!' cried Galeran, as he pulled the boy towards him.

A set of horses hauling a cart of stone cut from the nearby quarries came blustering into the square in a cloud of dust. It thundered by leaving both knight and boy covered in fine white powder.

'I am looking for a friend,' replied Galeran, dusting himself off and grinning at the boy as he did the same. 'A master glazier by the name of Audouard. Do you perchance know him?'

'No, Sir, I think not. How much will you pay me to look after your mount?'

'Enough to buy yourself a few of those oublies dipped in honey,' said the knight, pointing to a nearby street-hawker.

'Done!' said the boy, stretching out his hand. 'I shall mind both your horse and your equipment. The master glaziers work over there,' he added, pointing out a group of wooden huts to the right of one of the towers. 'What's your horse called?'

'Quolibet. He is from a monastery in Flanders and the like of him you won't see in these parts. So, boy, look after him well. And you, be calm,' the knight ordered as he stroked his old friend's neck.

Galeran went towards the wooden huts. Obscene drawings and slogans in crude handwriting covered the light wood of the palisade. The knight let out a long whistle as he read one of the lines.

'I am but a fickle thing. In my heart I possess the women I may not touch. I shall go to my death with a drink in my hand. I seek pleasure sooner than eternal salvation, my soul is dead and I care only for the flesh.'

'Ah, you've spotted that one! Some goliard wrote it when our backs were turned. We shall have to remove it before the canons see it,' said a young worker who had followed the knight's gaze.

'I have seen the same sort of thing, if more poorly phrased, on the walls of Paris and Saint-Denis. With such remarks I can understand that these goliards are beginning to worry both King and bishops. Are there many of them here in Chartres?'

'We don't know, we rarely see the same ones twice. They go about in groups of four or five, sometimes more. They aren't too bad, mind you, even if they are bit too familiar with our women for our liking. It's at night, when they get blind drunk, that they're dangerous. In the morning we often find a few of them lying wounded in the street from a night's drunken brawling. The Provost's men are not at all keen on running into these lads after the curfew!'

'That I can understand, but at least it keeps them on their toes.'

'Indeed,' replied the worker with a laugh. 'May God protect you, Sir.'

'And you too.'

In the place to which the boy had pointed a group of apprentices in blue smocks were working with slim rods of lead. Two of them were carefully setting mottled plates of glass, which resembled mosaics, on long trestle tables.

A tall figure in a light-blue smock caught Galeran's eye. The man was directing his apprentices' work with a firm voice. As lean as an ascetic and still youthful, Master Audouard cut a striking figure. Passion showed itself in his every action.

Galeran watched him work for a moment, noting the obvious authority he had over his team. He approached the man and gave him a friendly tap on the shoulder. Audouard turned to find Galeran's radiant eyes looking into his own.

'Greetings, my friend.'

'Galeran! What joy!' said Audouard, throwing his arms around the knight. 'I hope you had a good journey. I was worried the fords might be treacherous after last night's downpour.'

'No, I had no problems, neither too much rain nor any sign of marauders. After leaving Saint-Denis I went to Vaux-de-Cernay to visit a monk who is a friend of mine. Then I rode to Gallardon in the company of Marcabru. Do you remember him? He's the troubadour who wrote all those fine poems vaunting Queen Aliénor's beauty, while all the time gibing at her husband the King?'

'Yes, I remember the rascal! His passion for our Queen was not at all to her husband's liking. What became of the man?'

'The King simply chased him out of the court. He was lucky not to be thrown into the dungeon. But I had a very pleasant journey in his company, all the same. He has a good voice and a fine repertory of songs of Acquitaine. He stayed on at Gallardon but we may well see him here in Chartres before long. Otherwise, I found the roads safer even than in my homeland. The villains must be resting. The paths have held up well under the rain. But I own I did not regret leaving the forest for the open fields and the spring sunshine.'

The midday Angelus bell was sounded and the workers prepared to take some refreshment. Planks laid across stones served as tables. The men of the chapter distributed the victuals: rye bread, bean soup, onions, eggs. Wine was served from barrels and fowl were roasted on spits. The atmosphere was festive. The men threw dice and knucklebones on the ground, while children played at quoits and other games as they waited for their mothers to call them in for their dinner.

'Come, let us celebrate our reunion!' said Audouard. 'I shall take you to my favourite inn.'

'Wait, I must fetch my horse. I left him with a boy who looks like he will one day make an honest man.'

Galeran could easily make out the impassive silhouette of Quolibet from a distance, and he smiled to see the little redhead standing next to the horse, stiff as a post and with an air of pride and concentration.

'Hey, boy! This is for you. I thank you.'

'Thank you, Sir!' said the boy, pocketing the small coin. 'Perchance I can be of further use to you. Do you need a guide to show you around Chartres? What about a pigeon? See how fat he is.'

'Fat he certainly is. Where did you find him?'

'I shot him as he sat on one of the towers of the cathedral. But don't tell the canons, they won't like it.'

'I see you are a boy with much mettle in you,' said Galeran with a smile. 'But be careful, for I think the workers would not appreciate you firing off your arrows around here, even if you were to tell them just how tasty are the pigeons that nest right beside them! But in answer to your question, no, I no longer require your services. You see, I've found my friend Audouard. He shall be my guide.'

The boy pouted, disappointed, then looked at Audouard. The master glazier stared back at him, frowning.

'You're Ausanne's brother, are you not? Your mother must be worried about you.'

'I am doing nothing wrong, Sir, and besides, I was about to leave,' said the boy, and ran off.

'You know him?'

'Yes. It is hard to forget somebody with hair that colour. They're all like Danes in his family. He's the youngest of a family of weavers. A good little chap but a headache for his father, who wants him to become an artisan like himself. But the boy spends his days shooting pigeons and fishing in the river. He's a crafty little devil who will always get by, but he thinks he has nothing to learn.'

7

Galeran took Quolibet by the bridle and followed Audouard to Place de l'Étape au Vin. They stopped in front of a pleasant building made with clay and chopped straw mortar that housed the Coeur Couronné rotisserie. On a long wooden table sat a barrel ringed with hoops of iron. A portly man, a crier by trade, called out to the passers-by, while another sold wine which customers could either take away with them in earthenware jugs or drink in the rotisserie. Galeran could not help but smile at the crier's patter:

'Come in, ye hot and thirsty men, come in. The wine here is good, the capons well browned. Come and taste wine from the Loire and from Bordeaux, come try our chicken, whose breast is more succulent than a woman's. Come in, come in.'

And then, in a quieter voice: 'Good day, Master Audouard, your table is ready. Oyez! Oyez! Oyez! Come in, ye hot and thirsty men . . . !'

'Good day, Ambroise,' said the glazier. 'Wait here a moment, Galeran. I shall see about your horse. I'll bet the stable here is almost as good as the inn itself!'

Audouard disappeared inside the building to return with the innkeeper's son.

'Let me take your mount, Sir,' said the young man. 'The stable is in a lane at the back.'

Galeran thanked the boy and removed his bags and his weapons from the horse.

Audouard pushed open the door of the rotisserie and stood aside to let the knight pass. The room they entered was dark and warm. A boy slowly turned a spit heavy with partridges and capons, while another, grave-faced, caught the fat that oozed out of the roasting fowl and poured it back over them.

The flames from the fire lit up the customers' cheerful faces. Students and workers sat at a large communal table and shared bread, onion soup and a jug of wine. The room was full of laughter and bawdy jokes. The floor, made of beaten earth, was strewn with fresh leaves. The innkeeper, a fat, balding man, meekly watched the proceedings.

Audouard sat down with a proprietorial air at a table next to the inn's only window. The serving girl, a blonde-haired lass with a complexion as clear as her bosom was generous, placed two jugs of the fragrant red wine on the table in front of them. She blushed when Galeran looked at her, then moved off to serve other customers.

'A fine tavern, my friend, and a pretty girl to serve us. A judicious choice. But tell me, where do you and your sister live? And tell me also about that which is closest to your heart, here as in Saint-Denis. How is your work progressing?'

'I am nearly halfway there with the commission, and a splendid subject it is! A Jesse tree. And I have finally found my blue; it is a very pure blue with a hint of green. Extraordinary!' exclaimed Audouard, whose joy at finding a listener who understood his quest for beauty had made him forget the knight's first question.

He paused for a moment's reflection, then continued with fervour.

'A blue as rich as the day, fragile as a flower in a field. I shall show you my sketches. No, better still, I shall take you up the scaffolding and you'll be able to see my work in a proper light.'

'Nothing would give me more pleasure.'

'My friend, I have been thinking about this blue for many a year. I had hoped to find it at Saint-Denis, but the cold light there worked against me. Here it is different, the light on the hill, the gentleness of the countryside, this blue all around. It reminds me of the Loire of my childhood. Mind you, the days seem too short and sometimes I wish the sun would never set.'

'Well do I understand you. Many a master craftsman has your tenacity. But you look exhausted. Shall we eat?'

The serving girl had placed before them bread and a clay plate with steaming chunks of goat meat garnished with onions and spices.

'Eat, my friend,' said Galeran. 'Is there something on your mind? Or perhaps your good sister Hermine is not looking after you properly any more?'

'Oh, no. She would be vexed if she heard you. The truth is

that these stained-glass windows have taken up all my time and perhaps my strength and vigour, too. But it is worth it, that I can assure you. To answer your question: yes, I do have a few worries. We have had several accidents here at the cathedral. Minor accidents, yet unusual. But more of this anon.'

He helped himself to a large piece of meat. Galeran cut some bread upon which he placed some meat.

'How is our dear Hermine?' he asked. 'Is she still as good a cook as ever?'

'You speak of her as though she were but a maid! She'll soon be fifty, you know! She's fit as a fiddle, even if her absent-mindedness is getting worse. The other day she wanted to make me a roast, but she forgot to light the fire! Imagine the look on my face when I went to carve it!'

Galeran smiled. He could well imagine Hermine serving her brother the raw meat with her usual calm.

'You shall see her after we've eaten. We live in a fine house which Bishop Geoffroy de Lèves lent us upon Abbé Suger's recommendation.'

'Is Geoffroy de Lèves still in charge of the school of Chartres?'

'No, Thierry has been chancellor for the last four years. He is perhaps not as renowned as his predecessor Yves, but the school is still famous, especially for its teaching of mathematics.'

'It would please me to attend a few lectures. Perhaps you could introduce me to the man?'

'I can do that tomorrow if you wish. But tell me, how long are you planning to stay in Chartres?'

'Five or six days, for then I must continue on. I have been summoned to the court of Blois by Thibaud IV.'

'I see you are still far from finding the solitude you seek. And not only for sordid affairs, I hope, for in Saint-Denis that was a vile and cruel business you had to attend to.'

Galeran looked his friend in the eye for a moment. A strange smile played on his lips as he replied.

'You know that I have declined all honours, and even went as far as turning down offers from the King and Queen. I should have joined the Cistercians a long time ago. Yet it is true that I am well-rooted in the here and now of this century. I still take pleasure in drawing my sword, in riding or in solving mysteries. I uncover villainy and baseness, but it is a game that I enjoy. There are too many evil-doers convinced that they can escape God's judgement. And besides, the monastic life would mean that I would have to forego certain pleasures that are all too dear to me!'

'That is only natural, by my faith,' said Audouard with a laugh. 'Does your strange dream still come to you?'

'Yes. Do you recall the evening in Saint-Denis when I first told you of it? That strange fountain made of yellow stone, with runes carved on it that I could not read, and that woman, whose only clothing was her hair, walking towards me and disappearing the moment I went to touch her. A dream, yes, but one so real and so frequent. Perhaps it is the only true reason why I travel the world. Perhaps my real quest is to find this woman.'

'You must try to break that spell. But tell me of Paris, of Aliénor and Louis.'

'Rumour has it their marriage is not going well. The entente between the two is said not to be too cordial.'

'Why is that?'

'Our lovely Queen and the King, whom some like to call "the monk", are much too different. And also, Aliénor has not yet given birth to a future king of France.'

'They are still young, that will come. Aliénor is too much of a woman not to be able to bear a child.'

'Not everyone has such an optimistic view of the matter, not least the Queen Mother.'

'It hardly surprises me that Adélaïde de Savoie, whom you know to be rigid and cold, does not care for Aliénor's exuberance. But then, does any woman like her daughter-in-law? It is impossible for them to be friends, perhaps not even desirable. And our old friend Abbé Suger, what has become of him?'

'He has hardly changed. Despite his low size and his poor health, he is still a giant among men. Last June he inaugurated his cathedral. It was the eleventh day of June. You had already left, had you not?'

'Yes, we arrived here last May. How was the famous ceremony?'

'Spectacular! Even if the Abbé is a little too fond of pomp and circumstance, not to mention gold, for my taste. I prefer the austerity of the Cistercians or of Bernard de Clairvaux. But it is true, never were there so many people on the road to Saint-Denis as on that day. As for our King, he made quite an entrance. His wife and his vassals wore their regalia, but the King himself wore only a penitent's tunic and a simple pair of leather sandals.'

'Why such a strange costume for the Master of the Kingdom of France?'

'Our King worries me. He has never been the same since the siege of Vitry-en-Perthois. Have you heard tell of it? Louis is indeed more like a monk than a warrior king. When he saw his soldiers, his own soldiers burning down houses, when he saw the church, where the townspeople had taken refuge, in turn going up in flames and collapsing on the poor wretches, they say he threw himself to the ground to beg for God's mercy. They say he lay there on that cursed hill, his face to the earth, for days on end.'

'Well can I believe it. What a burden on the conscience! A church is a sacred place. I have heard that Bernard de Clairvaux reminded Louis of this in the most severe fashion.'

By the time the Angelus bell summoned the men back to work, the two friends had done justice to the innkeeper's culinary offerings and his excellent wine. Audouard chattered gaily in a jaunty tone that contrasted singularly with his austere appearance. The pair headed off, arm in arm, towards Rue au Lait where the master glazier and his sister lived.

8

A delightful smell of honey wafted past their noses as soon as the two men pushed open the heavy oak door. The modest wattle-and-daub house had a pleasant communal room – a corner of which was used as the kitchen – with a pretty stone fireplace, two tiny bedrooms, and outside a lavatory and a garden, which was Hermine's favourite place and where she would bask in the sun whenever it deigned to show itself.

A large trestle table, some stools, a chair, a dresser, and a chest for the linen were all the furnishings the communal room contained.

The kitchen clearly belonged to a woman who loved life's good and beautiful things. Casseroles and clay dishes hung on the walls and a stone basin served for preparing food and for washing. Bees buzzed around a dozen stone pots filled with preserves that sat cooling on a shelf. On a credence table lay plates of Italian ceramic, some cutlery and two cups. A pair of fat hams and chunks of bacon hung above a butcher's block. A barrel of wine was perched on a rough-hewn wooden stool in a corner of the room. A bouquet of meadow flowers bloomed in a stoneware vase.

But of Hermine there was no trace.

'Hush!' said Audouard to Galeran as he pointed out through the half-open door to his sister sitting in the sun.

She was sitting sewing on a stone bench in the herb garden. Next to her sat a fat tabby cat, which stopped licking its paws and stared at the visitors for a moment before gracefully jumping to the ground and slinking off.

The woman was of imposing girth, with a gentle, round face that was prettily wrinkled. Her half-undone headdress and her precariously balanced bun of white hair suggested she had forgotten how to use a comb. Her stained smock added to her air of distraction. She bent over her work, embroidering the master glazier's initials on a bedsheet.

'Good day to you, sweet Hermine,' said Galeran, planting a

resounding kiss on the old woman's cheek. 'I have missed you.'

Hermine gave a start and then turned crimson at the sight of the knight.

'Oh, it's you, Chevalier Galeran! I didn't hear you come in. I wasn't expecting you so early.'

'I thank you and ask you to forgive us for having surprised you. The temptation was too strong! Your pretty house is as charming as your own dear person. I see you have made some preserves, just as you used to in Saint-Denis.'

'Galeran, that will do,' said Audouard. 'You will have plenty of time later to make my sister blush. Come, I shall show you your room, which we shall be sharing. You'll note how fresh and clean the bedding is.'

'Farewell, Hermine,' said Galeran. 'I shall return to tell you all the gossip from the court and a few of the love stories you so like to hear.'

Audouard pushed open a double door made of oak. The room they entered was also simply furnished. It contained a large chest made from pear wood, a bed and two stools. There was but one note of colour: a fragment of stained glass, hung in front of the room's only window, representing an angel with its wings spread and its hands clasped in a gesture of peace and mercy. Galeran looked silently at the figure for a moment, then unpacked his bags and placed his clothes in the large wooden chest. His eye paused gratefully on the thick, wadded bedcover. He was more than happy to exchange the guardroom at Gallardon and the nights in the open air for the comfort of this little room.

'Yours is decidedly a hospitable house. The stained glass is your work, is it not?'

'Yes. But it is merely a study. I wanted to try working with orange glass. The figure of the angel seemed so natural among the flames. But I must leave you now. Hermine has prepared a bath for you. You are in good hands here. Get settled in, have a stroll around the town and then come and find me at the cathedral at Vespers. I must go, my workers await me. Farewell, my friend.'

'Thank you, Audouard, for your hospitality.'

Hermine came into the room.

'The water is hot, Sir, and the tub is ready. I shall be in the garden if you need me.'

'Thank you, sweet Hermine, I shall join you when I have washed.'

The knight went into the warm communal room. For once, Hermine had thought of everything. A fire blazed in the hearth and steam rose up from a large wooden tub filled with boiling water. Neatly folded towels lay on the linen chest. Galeran laid down his sword, piled his clothes on a stool by the fireplace and slid rapturously into the thyme-scented water. A thick flannel covered the bottom of the tub to protect him from splinters. The room was soon filled with steam. The logs in the fire crackled, and the din of the town seemed muffled by the tranquillity of the place. The knight stretched his stiff muscles and vigorously rubbed himself down with a horsehair brush. He washed away the dust of the road and the fatigue that had dulled his body during his long days in the saddle. He examined his long, muscular limbs, and contemplated the terrible scars on his left side that ached at night whenever the weather changed.

'I have seen worse!' he thought. 'How many of my fellows have scars that seep pus and never heal? And, after all, my essential parts are safe!' he ruminated, casting his eyes down towards his virility.

It was some time before Galeran could extract himself from the tub. He energetically dried himself off, then put on his linen shirt, his breeches, his coat of mail, and his tunic. He placed his sword back in his baldric, took his pouch and went to see Hermine. She had returned to her favourite bench and now sat slumped upon it, asleep and with her face fallen into her embroidery. Galeran watched her for a moment, a tender smile on his lips, and then quietly made his way out into the street. The day was fine and warm, the streets teemed with people. Galeran walked swiftly and with a determined air towards the upper town.

9

It was difficult to make any progress through Rue aux Drapiers. There was a succession of metal and wood signs, each vaunting the merits of the various artisans. Stallholders hailed the passers-by, each praising his goods more loudly than the next. The townsfolk marched by, some intent on making a purchase, others merely curious. They stopped to examine sheets, to feel a roll of cloth, measure some material, or merely to chat. Money passed from one purse to another. Galeran stopped a few times to look at the drapers' stalls for which the town was famous, and then decided to turn back towards the cathedral. After many detours through the narrow streets he arrived at the ramparts behind the sanctuary. From here he had a magnificent view over the fields and the forest. His eye roved over the curves of the pitched roofs and out to the countryside beyond before coming to rest on the shining river that flowed below the town.

A young worker struck up a song in his fine tenor's voice:

Westron wind, when will thou blow?
The small rain down can rain.
Christ, that my love were in my arms,
And I in my bed again.

A man stopped to give ear, then a washerwoman, then a few schoolboys. Galeran found himself in the midst of a group of admiring listeners. The air was taken up by a child, then by all in the circle. The workers high up in the cathedral responded with their own chants. When the young workman's voice finally faded, an approving murmur ran through the crowd. But the hot afternoon sun soon chased them from the esplanade.

Galeran applauded the young singer and made off towards an inn he had spotted near the cathedral on Rue Fulbert. A sign gave the tavern's name as the Rovin Vignon, and a few tables under a wooden canopy welcomed the thirsty. The knight took a seat near a table at which sat two hearty fellows deep in conversation.

'We have to t-tell the p-p-p-Provost,' Galeran heard one of them say.

'Let us wait a little longer,' said his companion. 'You know how easily our master loses his temper. And the Provost is not the most gentle of men. He'll think we were behind it.'

The men's nervous disposition held the knight's attention.

'B-but Robert, it doesn't l-look like he s-spent the night here. That's n-n-not n-n-n-normal. We should be on the w-way to B-B-Blois by now.'

'Look, you might want to get hauled over the coals, but I don't!'

'You th-think he's taken the st-stones with him? If something h-happens to him, they'll w-w-w-wonder w-why we didn't tell the p-p-Provost.'

'Oh, calm down, Gilles. Have some more wine. If he hasn't appeared by tonight we shall go and see the Provost.'

'P-promise?'

'Promise,' said his accomplice, spitting on the ground to seal the deal.

Galeran paid no more attention to the men. The innkeeper, a robust chap with a hard face, had come out to serve him.

'Do you wish to eat or drink?'

'Some cold wine will do the trick,' replied the knight.

Just then a young woman, dressed in a heavy green robe and with her face veiled, brushed against him as she entered the inn. He had just enough time to glimpse her bustier and the fine batiste of the veil that evoked the slender line of her neck and the whiteness of her skin. The woman marched up to the innkeeper, talked to him animatedly and left again as quickly as she had come in, mingling into the passing crowd.

'A true beauty,' thought Galeran as he watched her disappear. 'Although a little out of place here. Why would such a woman have dealings with an innkeeper?'

The innkeeper, propped up against the door, also longingly watched the gracious form move off into the distance.

A frail serving girl brusquely placed a cup of light red wine in front of the knight. He drank it slowly, paid, and began walking towards the Hôtel-Dieu. A hawker overburdened with goods came straight at him, and as he moved to one side he collided with a young woman.

'Pardon me, my lady! Have I hurt you? I am grieved.'

The woman smiled and gave him an amused look. Her pale complexion was dotted with freckles, her head crowned with long plaits of russet hair. She looked at him for another moment before replying.

'No harm has been done, Sir. And besides, it was not your fault.'

She turned and walked off without waiting for a response. She was already lost in the throng before the knight could say or do anything.

'Hmmm! My encounters today are happy and frequent, but a little too short for my liking.' He sighed with feigned resignation.

The bells announcing Vespers began to ring out as he arrived at the foot of the cathedral. The sun, an enormous ball of molten metal, was dropping towards the horizon. The stone sculptures now seemed independent of the cathedral, their forms emphasised by the radiance of the setting sun.

Work on the site had stopped. The last workers, stonecutters, glaziers and carpenters were nimbly climbing down ladders, their voices mingling in the evening air. After the heat of the day, the men were glad to return to the cool of the little streets. On the ground others were putting away hods and barrows, tools were gathered up and carefully cleaned before being stored in sheds. Masons washed themselves in stone troughs filled with icy water.

Galeran went towards one of the towers to seek out Audouard's long silhouette. He did not find it and was about to turn back when a cry of terror made him look up.

A dark shadow was hurtling towards him. The knight sprang back just in time to avoid the body that crashed to the ground beside him with a horrible thud. At the same moment – as every day at this time – the great bell of Notre Dame swang into motion, calling the faithful to prayer. Within a few seconds the acrid smell of viscera and blood filled the air and

Galeran had to overcome his nausea before kneeling down to examine the broken figure.

The man was no more than a bloody lump from which emerged tufts of black hair. Only his hands had remained somehow intact in the midst of this sticky mass of broken limbs.

Terror-stricken workers began running around and shouting, fearing that building materials were falling from the edifice. Panic spread throughout the site. A stonemason ran and fetched the master foreman. He quickly arrived on the scene, ordered torches to be lit, and restored calm with but a few words of his powerful voice.

Galeran had often encountered death, but found it difficult to remain impassive before the remains of this unfortunate. His face pallid, he stood up again as Audouard arrived and gave a sign to his men to move back from the dead body.

'There is nothing we can do,' said Audouard. 'He is dead.'

''Tis Jérôme,' said a worker, a young mason whose face was deathly pale.

'How can you tell?' asked Galeran, covering up the corpse with a white cloth the young man handed him.

'I know him, and I recognise his ring,' he answered, pointing to a wedding ring on one of the dead man's fingers.

The mason turned away and began to vomit. A colleague rushed to him and helped him away from the scene.

'And you, Audouard, do you know him?' asked the knight, turning towards his friend.

The master glazier stood transfixed, staring up at the tower.

'What is it, Audouard?'

Galeran also looked up. He thought he saw a silhouette on the walkway from which the worker had fallen. He rubbed his eyes, unsure of himself, and when he looked again there was nothing to be seen there in the fading light. Audouard stood impervious to all around him, gazing up at the cathedral, lost in thought.

Galeran led him gently aside.

'Do you know him? Audouard, what is going on?' he asked.

'Nothing. Let us go, there is nothing more we can do for the boy. The men-at-arms will soon be here,' said Audouard, crossing himself. 'Look! The priest has come to give the last rites.'

An old clergyman knelt by the body. The murmur of the workers' prayers for their dead companion was heard throughout the cathedral.

A pensive Galeran moved off alongside his friend.

'Is this the sort of accident you spoke of today in the inn?'

'No. Until now nobody had been killed,' Audouard said, with a note of hesitation in his voice that did not escape Galeran. 'But on Friday, one of the carpenters working on the spire came very close to death. A stone apparently came loose above him. The master foreman has had the scaffolding strengthened since then, he makes the men rope themselves together when they're working on the higher parts, and he has had some guardrails put up. But apart from that there has been nothing very serious until today.'

'Come, my friend, you look shaken. Let us go to Ambroise's for a jug of wine. You could do with it, and so could I.'

'I'm feeling better, I assure you.'

'Your face does not match your words. I must own that I, too, was sickened at the sight of the corpse.'

A lively fire and a few torches along the walls lit up the inn. The news from the cathedral had not yet reached the tavern, and the customers drank and talked merrily. Despite his paunch, the innkeeper moved nimbly around the room as he served his guests. The two friends sat at a table and ordered a jug of the local wine. Audouard sat silently, cup in hand. Galeran watched him, and it was some time before any words were exchanged. The wine eventually brought some colour back to the glazier's face.

'Forgive me, I am poor company,' he said.

'There is something you are not telling me. This death, horrible as it was, should not have had such an effect on you. This type of accident is commonplace in this line of work. Unless, of course, you think it was no accident.'

'No, Galeran, no!' protested Audouard. 'What are you saying?'

'Nothing. But I know you too well. Your reaction to what we have just seen is not normal.'

The glazier's face hardened.

'You are mistaken, I assure you.'

'Very well, my friend, let us speak no more of it. I did not seek to offend you. Shall we go home to your sweet sister?'

'Yes, she'll be waiting for us.'

10

They paid for the wine, lit a torch they had borrowed from the innkeeper and made their way towards Audouard's house.

The Provost's men were putting up chains across the roads, a simple device used to stop brigands escaping on horseback. Silence fell over the town. Torches propped up in stone recesses illuminated the little statues of the Virgin Mary that dotted the streets. The two friends reached home without incident and sat down to the supper Hermine had prepared for them, a delicious soup and a *taillis aux épices*. A fire blazed in the hearth, and a small oil lamp lit up the table. Hermine had hoped for some saucy story before bedtime but was disappointed to see the men eat their meal with barely a word. She served them their grog, a mixture of hot wine and milk, then took her leave, kissing her brother on the cheek before she went to bed.

Audouard, exhausted after the long day, meticulously cleaned his glazier's diamond, his chisel and his compass, put them away in his leather satchel, and said good night to Galeran. After a brief visit to the lavatory, the knight washed his hands and then joined his friend. Audouard lay facing the wall and appeared to be asleep. Galeran took off his clothes and slipped into the bed that Hermine had dried out with warm bricks from the fire. He reflected a while on the tumultuous day and on his friend's strange disposition. Then he fell into a sleep that was troubled by images of the dark shadow hurtling towards him from above. He sat up suddenly and tried to recall each instant, from the cry of terror till the moment when the poor unfortunate lay crushed at his feet. But it was above all Audouard's face and its disturbing pallor that was etched on the knight's memory.

Why? Oh God, why am I not dead? Why do I live and not him? I did not seek his death. He forced me to kill him. He threatened to reveal everything. I could not accept this, I had to be near her. They would have put me in prison. I had to kill him, Lord, I swear I had no choice. I am not well, my hand burns. It is not me, Lord, it is this hand of mine, this hand that has already lit the stake at which my beloved will be burned. Why, why? My God, have mercy on me. Let me die. I can't go on.

PART TWO

Though we live in darkness, we know the light . . . being in death, we know life.

Catherine of Siena

11

A soft tapping on the wooden door woke Galeran. The knight leaped from his bed in nature's garb and flung open the door, thinking it was Audouard who had knocked. But it was Hermine who stood before him, and she gave a little gasp at the sight of his exposed manhood. Galeran pulled on his breeches and a linen shirt.

'Pardon me, gentle Hermine. I thought it was your brother.'

'Your breakfast is ready, Sir,' she said, suppressing a smile. 'My brother has already left for his atelier. He would like you to join him there at Sext.'

'That will please me well. But let us first breakfast together. My bed was so comfortable that I slept like a log. I didn't even hear the morning Angelus.'

Hermine led him to the communal room where she had laid out on the table a bowl of goat's milk, a jug of wine, a loaf of bread wrapped up in a cloth, some sausages, and some cheese.

'The sight of this feast has suddenly made me ravenous,' said Galeran as he drew up a stool and placed chunks of sausage and cheese on a slice of bread.

'What is this?' he asked, pointing to a small clay pot.

'Rose honey. A friend of Audouard who was in the Orient taught me how to make it. Eat, dear knight, it is good. And try some of this, too.'

From underneath a cloth she took out a fine ham and handed it to the knight.

'I thank you, Hermine. What sort of weather have we today?'

'It was hazy when I rose this morning, but it was the sort of haze that heralds sun and heat.'

Galeran cut himself a last slice of bread, took a final drink of wine, stretched, and smiled at the old woman, who watched him out of the corner of her eye to make sure he had everything he needed.

'Hermine, I know of no one whose fare is as good as yours.'

He kissed her on the forehead, causing her to blush, and

went to wash himself in the tub in the garden. A vague sadness had come over him, and neither the splendour of the morning sky nor the cool water he poured over his body could chase the feeling away.

'Living in town changes many things,' he mused. 'It seems that the closer people live together, the less they know each other. They hide and protect themselves from each other, even from those for whom they feel affection. They are like towns, with ramparts all around them. Once Hermine would have been no more ashamed to look at my virility than a new-born child. And this manner of hiding the place where one sleeps. Is the large, communal bed not the finest thing about a hospitable home? Yes, one might say that townspeople are inventing shame.'

The streets of Chartres were already teeming with people by the time the knight left Audouard's dwelling. The morning haze had gone and the sky was cloudless. The smell of wood fires and of cooking filled the air. A little merchant woman sang as she walked by, bearing on her hips a large wicker basket brimming with carrots and beans. Pigs hunting for food ran about the roads, shadowed by marauding cats and dogs. Hawkers were trying out their patter on passing women. Few could resist these tempters whose honeyed speech was sprinkled with homages to the beauty of women and to their fine tastes. Their goods – ribbons, buttons, lace, yarn, cloth, and passementerie – were displayed in strange wooden crates which hung from their necks on broad leather straps. These men often came from the high mountains. Bearing their wares on their back, they would cross Flanders, France or Italy to do their buying and selling. They returned home but once a year, a little money in their pocket, to visit the patient families who could never know whether they would ever again see them alive.

12

His stained brown cloak fixed tightly over his shoulders, his cloth bag in hand, Bastien 'the Weasel' took a final, careful look between the broken laths of his shelter and decided to leave the lean-to.

The Weasel's evening had been eventful. Chased by the men-at-arms for making a racket after curfew, he had taken refuge in this hut used for storing wood. He had spent the night there, as drunk as if he had fallen open-mouthed into a barrel of wine. His red nose planted in the middle of his face like a beacon, his three remaining hairs standing like spikes atop his head, Bastien set out to find a quiet place where he could sleep off his hangover. He crossed Rue de la Juiverie, scrambled through some bushes to reach the banks of the Eure, and lay down in the grass. Lulled by the sound of the water, the old wastrel soon drifted off.

The sun was already high when he woke. He stretched, yawned, and decided it was time for some food. His stomach gave a peculiar rumble to remind him that he had not eaten since the previous evening. He was gathering up his old rags when he spotted it. The body of a man, jammed against a tree trunk that floated next to the bank, rose and fell with the river. The corpse was naked, and its head knocked against the stump with a dull and regular thump.

The Weasel's bloodshot eyes stared at the dead man as he tried to calm himself with the thought that this was, after all, no more than a cadaver.

'No doubting the chap's dead. Don't even need to look twice to see that. I likes the dead better, I do,' he thought. 'They be nice and quiet, not like the living ones who spend their time chasing after me. But with my luck these days, I reckon I'll be better off pretending I saw nothing.'

He made to leave the scene, but at that very moment two boys hunting for frogs and snails burst through the bushes next to him. In one glance they saw both the Weasel turning on his heels and the naked body jammed against the tree trunk.

'Help! Help! There's a man drowning!' cried the younger of the two.

'Can't you see he's dead?' cried the second, a blond boy with a wily air about him and a pointed little nose. 'Hey! Old man! Come back! Help us get him out of the water.'

But the Weasel kept running towards the town. As he turned into an alleyway he ran into an old acquaintance, Sergeant Geoffroy, one of the Provost's men.

'Well, well,' said the sergeant, grabbing him by the collar, 'you're still running, my friend. We must have made such an impression on you last night that you haven't stopped. Come with me so you can have a little rest in the nice, quiet cellar in the Prévôté!'

'But Sergeant, I was looking for you,' the Weasel protested vehemently. 'There's a body in the river, near Rue de la Juiverie. We need help to get him out.'

'What's that you're saying? More of your usual palaver, eh?'

'I swear on it,' said the old beggar. 'Come and see, two boys are there with the man.'

'If you're lying, Weasel, you'll regret it,' said the sergeant, who still had a tight grip on the man's cloak. 'Right then, show me the way!'

A small crowd had already gathered around the corpse by the time the two men reached the scene. The boys' shouts had brought some workers who had been fulling cloth a little further along the river. They had managed, with the help of a pole, to dislodge the body and heave it up onto the bank.

'Move aside,' said the sergeant as he leaned over the cadaver.

A glance at the bloodless face persuaded him that there was nothing more that could be done to help the unfortunate.

'Hey, Sergeant, that man ran away when we arrived,' said the blond boy, pointing an accusatory finger at the Weasel. 'And he wouldn't help us.'

'Ran away? Me? I was only going to fetch the Sergeant,' protested the Weasel.

Sergeant Geoffroy knitted his thickset brows.

'I shall have to speak of this with the Provost. There is something fishy here.'

Then he addressed the workers.

'Can one of you go and fetch some of my men at the Prévôté? And you, Weasel, don't you budge till we decide what to do with you.'

13

'I'll take some of that, if you please,' Galeran told the draper, pointing to one of the long rolls. 'It is fine material. You deserve your reputation, friend.'

'Our town is rightly celebrated for the quality of its fabrics!'

As he spoke, the man unrolled the fine batiste on a long wooden table. He swiftly made two marks with a pencil, cut the cloth and handed it to Galeran. The knight reached for his pouch, paid his due and put the material, which he planned to give as a tablecloth to Hermine, in his satchel.

Rue aux Drapiers was not the widest of streets, and was rendered even narrower by the merchants' tables. As Galeran turned to leave the stall with his purchase he bumped into a young woman hurrying along the street. She gave a little cry of both pain and surprise.

'A thousand pardons, madam! But tell me, have I not already had the honour?' asked Galeran as he looked at the pretty redhead he had encountered the previous day.

'Forgive my frankness, but I would prefer not to have made your acquaintance at all! By my faith, I find you a little too direct,' said the young woman, grimacing with pain.

'Have I hurt you?' enquired Galeran.

'I must have twisted my ankle a little.'

Then she looked down at the ground and saw that her satchel had been flung open and her tools scattered across the street.

'Let me help,' said Galeran, bending down to gather up the fine metal tools. 'These are surgical instruments. Are you a physician?'

His head slightly to one side, the knight stared at the young woman with his deep-blue eyes. She proudly held his gaze.

'Yes, Sir. I do what I can to cure men of their ills. And you, knight, do you also know the art of healing? Not many people would recognise these instruments.'

'Indeed, I have on occasion aided men of medicine. But

allow me to introduce myself,' he said, standing up and handing back her satchel. 'My name is Galeran de Lesneven.'

'Dame Ausanne, Sir.'

'It is a rare thing to meet a lady physician. Who was your teacher?'

'The disciple of another woman doctor, and a remarkable one at that. Dame Trotula of Salerno.'

'So you were in Italy?' said the astonished knight. 'Salerno is the most renowned of medical schools. They say it was founded by four physicians – a Greek, a Latin, a Jew and a Saracen – and that each taught in his own tongue!'

'You know more than I. Alas, I did not travel to Salerno. One of Dame Trotula's disciples lived for many years here in our town. He passed on his learning to me, and gave me copies of some manuscripts from Salerno. I also received some instruction from Pierre-Gilles de Corbeil. He resided here before moving to Paris. Have you heard tell of him?'

'Yes. Queen Aliénor was fond of the learned doctor. He must be an old man now. But permit me to congratulate you, madam, for you have managed, without ever leaving your home town, to acquire much knowledge.'

'And you . . . '

A man-at-arms suddenly appeared beside them and grabbed the astonished young woman by the arm before she could finish her sentence. Galeran did not appreciate the fellow's manners and prepared to step in.

'Dame Ausanne, follow me, I beg you,' said the man-at-arms. 'They've found a man in the Eure near Porte Guillaume and the Provost wants to see you immediately.'

'Is he still alive?'

'I think not.'

Galeran frowned as he listened to this exchange.

'You are limping, Dame Ausanne, and that is of my doing. Let me earn your forgiveness by carrying your satchel,' he said, and picked up the bag before Ausanne had time to respond.

A little redhead boy suddenly emerged from behind the young woman.

'Sister, please let me come too!'

'This is my brother Benoît,' Ausanne told Galeran.

'I know the knight already, sister,' said the boy proudly. 'I have even looked after his horse.'

'He speaks the truth, madam. I should have known that such hair could only come from one and the same family.' Galeran smiled as he looked at the boy's round, freckled face and the hazel eyes.

'That boy spends more time in the streets than at his work! Benoît, you must go back to the atelier now. One does not go to see a dead man, may his soul rest in peace, for entertainment. You are neglecting your weaving these days. Watch out, for Father may decide to apprentice you somewhere far away from us all.'

'I am not a child any more! And I don't like weaving. I want to become a cavalryman,' replied a sulky Benoît.

With that he turned on his heels and ran off.

'Please excuse my brother, he thinks only of weapons and horses. He is driving our family to despair. But I think it is the boy who will win out in the end, for he's crafty enough. Very well, Sir, you may accompany me. But we must hurry, for the Provost is not what one might call an easy fellow.'

The man-at-arms walked in front as they marched towards the Jewish quarter. Ausanne, whose ankle now appeared to be functioning normally, walked with a self-assurance that showed she knew these labyrinthine streets intimately.

14

A small figure followed after them, hiding in doorways and behind people strolling in the streets.

The three left Rue de la Juiverie near the synagogue and took a narrow passage which led them to a river bank covered in gorse and other bushes. They soon came to a crowd of people among whom they could see some men-at-arms as well as the Provost, who was easily distinguished by his large hat. Ausanne, suddenly serious, marched up to him and bowed her head gracefully.

'I salute you, Sir Provost.'

'Dame Ausanne, at last,' he replied gruffly, paying no heed to Galeran's bow. 'We found this man's body floating by the bank. I want you to tell me if his death was an accident or the result of foul doings.'

'Did you undress him?' asked Ausanne with some surprise.

'No, he was found like that.'

She knelt down by the corpse that lay face down on the ground. The man had been thin, with uniformly white skin that showed his life had not been one of physical labour, and he had a shock of grey hair. Galeran handed Ausanne's bag to her and moved to one side. But he kept his eyes on her, curious to see the woman at work.

The physician examined the body from the toes right up to the mud-spattered hair, through which she ran her slender fingers. She felt the stiff limbs and then asked a man-at-arms to turn the corpse over. When he did so, she brushed the hair from the dead man's face and gave a start at what she saw.

'What is it, Dame Ausanne?' asked the Provost.

'Do you know who this man is, Sir Provost?'

'No.'

'I do. He was one of my patients. A jeweller, I think, who was staying at the Rovin Vignon inn.'

'The place on Rue Fulbert? Strange, the innkeeper never

mentioned anyone being missing. And that Jehan is always coming to me with some gripe or other – already two of his customers have made off without paying. A jeweller, you say? No doubt there's a tale of greed and plunder here!'

'If I may, Sir Provost,' said Galeran, 'I know that the jeweller's two assistants were aware that he had gone missing. I overheard their talk in the very same inn yesterday afternoon. They wanted to tell you but feared your wrath even more than that of their own unfortunate master.'

'And who are you, Sir?' growled the Provost, annoyed at being interrupted by a stranger.

'Pardon me, Sir Provost, I would have introduced myself but you gave me no occasion to do so. I am Galeran de Lesneven, and I am on my way to the court of Blois.'

'Would you be a relative of Florent de Lesneven, the crusader?'

'You have heard tell of him? He was my grandfather.'

'Was?'

'He died in July 1099, killed by a Sudanese archer. It was the day the crusaders took Jerusalem. He was a liegeman of Godefroï de Bouillon.'

'A valiant knight and a fine warrior,' said a suddenly milder Provost. 'My father knew him well. He was present at his dubbing. But we shall speak of this later, if it pleases you. So, you say you heard a conversation which proves that this man was already missing yesterday? And did these men appear to have a guilty conscience?'

'No, I think they are not in any way connected with the death of their master. May I suggest that you have the banks upstream from this point searched for the old man's clothes? They may provide you with some clues.'

The young Benoît had been standing nearby during this conversation and had heard every word. He found the knight's idea a worthy one and decided that he himself would search for the clothes.

Bastien the Weasel, who sat on the ground with his head in his hands, gave an anguished sigh. The beggar was already weary of the whole affair. The Provost, having asked him a few questions, had lost interest in the man and had left him sitting there like an abandoned shoe. The sergeant, who was watching him out of the corner of his eye, called him over.

'You can clear off, Weasel! We have no more need of you. Go and take your filthy self elsewhere!'

The old man did not need to be told twice. He gathered up his rags and made off.

'And you, Dame Ausanne, what do you make of it all?' enquired the Provost as he turned to face the young woman.

'I know not what to think. All I can say is that I saw this man alive last week with his two assistants. He had a fever and his men took him to see me in Rue Percheronne.'

Ausanne calmly resumed her examination. She studied the dead man's face, his torso, his knees, his ankles, and when she had done she rose to her feet again with some difficulty, seemingly overcome with fatigue. She drew the Provost aside.

'The evidence suggests that this man, who had just recovered from a fever, was not going for a swim.'

'What do you mean?'

'He received a violent blow to the base of the skull which almost smashed the cranium. It was no weakling that delivered it.'

'Could it not have been the result of a fall? Or perhaps the tree trunk his body was jammed against?'

'I do not see how a fall could leave marks like that. And if the tree were the cause, then why are there no other such bruises on the body? No, I think not. This man was murdered. He lost much blood. There was but one blow, but it was a fatal one, and the man had breathed his last breath before he ever touched the water. If you will allow me to conduct a more thorough examination, I have no doubt that this will confirm my assessment.'

'Everything seems quite clear as it is. He definitely did not die from drowning?'

'Look, even if I put pressure on his body no water comes out. And you know that a drowned man is like a goatskin about to burst. Besides, there is something else that makes me think he was killed. Look at his wrists and his ankles. The skin has been cut into, and the blue marks you see there undoubtedly came from a rope. The poor man had no chance.'

'I shall have the body brought to the Prévôté. Can you finish your examination there this afternoon?'

'That is the best course of action, Sir Provost,' said Ausanne. 'Given the heat of the day and the state of the corpse, the wretch should be buried as quickly as possible. It would seem that the murder did not take place last night. It was more likely yesterday or even the day before, which would corroborate what Chevalier Galeran has said.'

'Very well. Let's have the banks of the river searched. Sergeant, get your men on the job and find me this man's belongings.'

The Provost then turned back to Ausanne.

'I thank you, madam, for your precious help. You may continue your examination in the judgement room, and there you will have more peace. And you, Sir, I would ask you to pardon my curtness, but that is how I am. I hope that in honour of your illustrious relative you will grace my table with your presence. That is an invitation I extend to Dame Ausanne.'

'That will indeed be an honour, Sir Provost,' said the knight as he turned on his heels and followed Ausanne, who was already making her way towards the upper town.

'Dame Ausanne, allow me to congratulate you for the swiftness and the clarity of your examination. You obviously have great talent, your hand is sure, and your judgement still surer.'

'I have no great merit,' replied Ausanne, blushing a little. 'I have simply had the misfortune to have examined several corpses. But your own judgement was equally sure.'

A half-smile played on the young woman's lips.

'Pray tell, you do not think highly of our Provost, do you?'

'I have met worse,' responded Galeran. 'Dame Ausanne, tell me, you seem very young to have encountered so many violent deaths.'

'It is a long and ugly story,' she replied, her pretty face suddenly sombre.

'Forgive me, I did not mean to upset you.'

'No harm has been done, Sir. But I must leave you now. I promised my family I would eat with them.'

'Very well. But please allow me to aid you in this affair. And, I beg you, assure me that I shall see you again.'

'I cannot say, Sir,' replied Ausanne, suddenly distant. 'But I shall consider it. Farewell, and take care.'

'Farewell, madam,' said Galeran.

He watched her stride away with a determined air, then headed for Notre Dame. There Audouard awaited him with an anxious look.

'Galeran, at last!'

'What is it, my friend? Why so worried?'

'I have been speaking to Jérôme's master. You know, the worker who fell to his death yesterday. He tells me something strange was going on. Jérôme left his work before the evening Angelus rang. He told his colleagues he had to meet a friend. His master says the chap often spoke of money problems. He had just got married and his young bride was costing him a lot more than he earned. The master thinks he may have borrowed money from one of his colleagues to keep his wife happy. And the rest you know.'

'But who is this myserious friend?'

'His colleagues say he is a stonecutter. But which one? There are about fifteen of them. And there is another thing. This morning one of my men found a walkway on the scaffolding smashed, as though it had been damaged by a storm. But the weather was fine last night, and when I saw the walkway yesterday evening it was in perfect condition! The men are getting frightened.'

'So you share my view that the mason's death was no accident? But who would have done such a thing? And why? You know the workers well. What do you think?'

The two men walked slowly away from the site. They said nothing for some time, each of them deep in thought. It was Galeran who eventually broke the silence.

'Audouard, you need to think over what has happened in this town, and particularly at the cathedral, since you arrived. And I beg you, if you have been hiding something, please tell me now.'

'I have hidden nothing of any consquence from you, Galeran. But you are right. I've been here for almost a year, and it was seven or eight months ago that these things began to happen. I didn't think about it much at the start. But now that a man has died and there are ever more accidents, I agree that we have to take the matter very seriously.'

'Think back. Was there any one single thing that marked the start of it all, or was it a number of things that you can now link together?'

'I honestly do not know. There were minor accidents, falls, materials broken, light injuries. As I told you yesterday.'

'Think again. I know there are a lot of comings and goings at the site, but did the master foreman recruit any new master craftsmen? Were there many voluntary workers on the site? Any strangers? Did you have any disputes about materials or animals?'

'No, I assure you, I . . . Well, yes, the master foreman did have problems with his suppliers of stone at the Berchères quarry. But it was nothing serious, and in the end it was amicably resolved. No, I can think of nothing of any importance. We did have a lot of people coming here from Saint-Denis, just like myself. The master foreman did have a very talented stonecutter who had been working on the church of Notre Dame de la Daurade in Toulouse. And, of course, we did take on a lot of voluntary workers.'

Audouard gave the knight a perplexed look, then sighed.

'I am afraid I am not much help to you.'

'Who knows? We shall have to find the answer, and it matters little how we do so. But are you sure there is nothing you wish to tell me?'

Audouard grew pale.

'No, Galeran, it is just that . . . Death and blood is not to my liking. The atmosphere here has been good – we all knew each other from Saint-Denis, or most of us – in any case, we had already worked together. And Thiberge, the master foreman, and his men, put so much effort into organising the building work.'

15

In the foreground was the countryside in full bloom. Its mix of forest, fields and rivers was dominated by a hill upon whose gentle slopes stood the town. Azure blue, bright red, and canary yellow were the threads of silk and wool that ran through Éloïse's slender fingers. The strong light of midday filtered through a narrow window into the little room where she worked. The tapestry was already strikingly beautiful, its forms and colours intensified by the beams of spring sunshine.

Éloïse, bent over her work, did not hear the bell calling her to table, and her brother Benoît was sent to fetch her.

'Come, Éloïse,' he said. 'We are all waiting for you. Ausanne is already there.'

Éloïse and her older sister had two things in common with the rest of their family – red hair and a passion for their art that nothing could suppress.

Éloïse stood up reluctantly, took a last look at her work, then followed Benoît to the communal room where her sister sat with her parents, brothers and uncles.

Ausanne was the only member of her family who had not chosen weaving as her profession. Nothing and nobody could make her change her mind. She had wanted to become a physician, and a physician she became. Her parents had at first opposed her choice. They wished her to follow in the family tradition, and they knew also that it was no easy thing for a woman to become a physician, particularly in a town like Chartres. The last physician, an old surgeon, had died in the Great Fire of 1134, and apart from a bonesetter who lived in Grand Beaulieu, there had been no one to replace him. But Ausanne was strong-willed, and was prepared to risk rejection by those closest to her. Faced with such determination, her parents eventually gave in.

Neither her family nor the inhabitants of Chartres and its environs ever had cause to regret her choice, for they found in her a devoted and, what is more, a very efficient doctor.

Ausanne was respected by all. She was gifted, she knew how to observe and rarely erred in her diagnosis.

She soon came to realise that in order to be better at her profession, she should make notes on each individual case she dealt with. She now always carried with her old rolls of paper on which she made her observations. Parchment being most expensive, she had managed to persuade the Bishop to permit her to use old parchment from the chapter-house. But she had to boil it or to soak it in lime before she could use it. She always had a large stock, which she stored in wicker baskets.

Éloïse's face lit up when she saw Ausanne. The two sisters spent far too little time together, in the view of the younger of the pair. Ausanne worked very hard, and would often spend several days in the leprosarium in Grand Beaulieu or in the villages around Chartres. Family meals were becoming a rarity, and Éloïse felt that the bond they had had as children was gone. She missed sharing a bed with her sister, and she missed the long walks they would take together, arm in arm, by the river.

'Ausanne, sweet sister, you look so well,' said Éloïse, kissing her on the lips.

'And you, Éloïse, are so pale. Mother,' said Ausanne, turning to Dame Isolde, 'you must watch over my little sister. She must get out more and she must eat more.'

'That I know, Ausanne, but you try talking reason to her. She is every bit as stubborn as you! I have given up. She thinks of nothing but weaving. You talk to her, she may listen to you.'

Ausanne sat on the long oak bench next to her sister, while Dame Isolde discreetly left for the communal room.

'You are very young, Éloïse, and very pretty. You must go out, take strolls by the river, meet some young men. It is springtime, my dear, so make the most of it. Spring is for the young.'

Oh, Ausanne! If they asked you to give up your work, what would you do?'

'No one is asking you to do that. But perhaps if you worked less, you might meet a fine young man, maybe even a handsome weaver.'

'If I meet a man who takes me away from my craft, I shall die.'

'What ideas you have in your pretty head! You really are working too much, I shall have to take you in hand myself.'

'That I would like,' said Éloïse with a mischievous smile, as she led her sister towards one of the two long trestle tables in the communal room.

The entire family, comprising a dozen men, women and children seated on wooden benches, joyously greeted the two sisters. The men chatted in loud voices, the women nodded wisely. Queen Aliénor was the main topic of conversation. The people of Chartres were expecting a visit from her, and the weaver family wanted to present her with a tapestry.

Silence fell on the room when the spit-roasted capons garnished with broad beans were brought in. The men, most of them young and strong, quickly tucked into the meat, cutting themselves large chunks of bread and frequently raising their pewter goblets to their lips.

When the repast was over the sisters, who had done more chatting than eating, placed some sweetmeats in the pewter *bonbonnière* the Bishop had given as a gift to the family. They made off with their spoils and sat on the stone bench in the garden.

'Ausanne, tell me, what have you been doing today?' asked Éloïse, her mouth full of sweetmeats.

'Today I met a very charming man, a Breton who goes by the name of Galeran de Lesneven. Or, if I am to be more precise, I made his acquaintance twice. And in a rather abrupt manner, I might add.'

'Oh, please tell!' said Éloïse, clapping her hands.

At which Ausanne told of her two encounters with the knight.

'What is he like? Is he handsome?'

'He is tall and slim. I hardly come up to his shoulder. When he looks at you, you have the rather troubling feeling that you have to tell him everything, even if you have nothing untoward to hide. His look pierces you.'

'What colour are his eyes?'

'Blue. And his voice is so gentle, tender almost. And . . . Oh, that's enough, let's speak no more of him. I shan't see him again. What about your work?' asked Ausanne, knowing that this was the only subject that might make her sister change the direction of their conversation.

'I started on the Bishop's commission four months ago and I'm making good progress. The cathedral inspires me. In fact, you might say that I am obsessed with it. But do tell me, Ausanne, do you like this young man?'

'Éloïse, you know well that nothing interests me but medicine.'

'Ausanne, can you not forget the past and think of yourself for once? You tell me to go out and enjoy myself, but perhaps you should practise what you preach. This is the first time in years that you have spoken to me about anything other than potions!'

'You exaggerate, sister. And anyway, I'm older than you, and I want no life other than the one I have. Oh, look at those little tits, aren't they pretty!' said Ausanne, pointing at the birds in another bid to change the subject.

The creatures chased each other with merry chirps and engaged in improbable acrobatics around a blossoming sweet-brier. The sisters watched for a while until Ausanne suggested that they pick some roses for their mother. They cut a few branches with a pair of scissors Éloïse kept in her belt before going back inside the house. Éloïse returned to her work, and Ausanne was soon joined by Benoît.

'Ausanne, Ausanne, can I come with you? Mother said I could. Please!'

Ausanne glared at him.

'You know how to sweet-talk women, don't you? Whether it's your mother, Éloïse or myself. Yes, you may, but you must promise to be good. You can help me prepare some remedies.'

'I promise I'll do as I'm told,' the boy replied gravely.

He then spoke in a much lower voice. 'I've found the dead man's clothes.'

'What?!'

'You heard me. I found the old man's clothes by the river.'

'You brat, Benoît, you lied to me! You followed us!'

'Don't get angry. I only wanted to help. Please, Ausanne!'

'Very well, but now you must do exactly as I tell you. I shall say goodbye to Mother and then we shall go to my office and we'll see what to do with you.'

Ausanne seized her little brother by the hand and led him off. She took her leave of her family and then went to Éloïse's atelier to kiss her goodbye. She opened the door quietly so as not to disturb her. When her eyes fell on the tapestry she stopped short.

The design was so beautiful that it seemed like an illumination. The cathedral was teeming with details that Ausanne had until now neither noticed nor even imagined. Éloïse sensed her sister's presence and turned to face her. She threw her arms around her neck and hugged her before she left.

As Ausanne strode away from her family home, she considered her brother and his fascination for weapons and chivalry. She recalled how brightly Benoît's eyes had shone as he sat of an evening and listened to the men telling tales of the Crusades. And how the boy, his cheeks aflame, had sworn to whoever cared to listen that he himself would one day go to Jerusalem or Antioch.

Benoît followed his sister in silence, a little worried to see her face so serious and knowing well that he was the focus of her thoughts.

16

Galeran was dining with Hermine and Audouard at their home on Rue au Lait. After the meal the two men went into the garden, where the knight tried to rid the glazier of his sombre humour.

'I must tell you about a charming little encounter I had this morning, Audouard.'

'Knowing you as I do, the word "charming" is a clear sign that it involved a woman,' said his friend, a hint of a smile on his lips. 'Did the lady tell you her name?'

'It involved a physician, and her name is . . . '

'Ausanne. Say no more. You do have good taste. She is beautiful, but she is also inaccessible, even for a man of your standing.'

'So you know her. But why do you say that?'

'Oh, it is a long story,' replied Audouard. 'But you can imagine that a girl as pretty as Ausanne would have many suitors.'

The knight's face darkened a little at these words.

'It is not what you think,' Audouard reassured him. 'Just one had any merit in her eyes. He was an apprentice stonecutter, a young chap with plenty of talent, who was working on the cathedral before the Great Fire of 1134.'

'The Great Fire?'

'It was on the fifth day of September. Most of the town was burned down, and the cathedral was very badly damaged. A terrible time. Even today people will not speak of it.

'At the time Ausanne must have been about fourteen, and she was in love with this man who was a couple of years older. They never found out how the fire was started. Ausanne, despite her great youth, proved herself to be a woman of action. She faced up to the tragedy with the courage and the tenacity that has since come to characterise her, and managed to save many children from the flames. I think it was that day that she found her vocation. As for her betrothed, he disappeared. We never found out what became of him. He may have perished, or he may have fled, like so many others, traumatised by the horror of the fire.'

'I think I now understand some of what she said today,' murmured Galeran. 'She told me she had seen many horrible deaths.'

'Eleven years have gone by and the most any man can boast is that she nursed him in sickness. She is respected and loved by all here in Chartres. But I am afraid you have little chance of making Ausanne deviate from the course she has set herself. She is as headstrong as yourself in many respects.'

'I have no intention of diverting her from her vocation. But it is true that she charmed me. And your tale has made me want to see her again even more.'

'Ah, my friend, you would do better to leave the woman well alone. She suffered greatly, but now she has found peace. Your company might not be good for her serenity. And take care not to confuse your own quest and your dreams with reality. This woman is very real, she is rooted in life and in her duty. She is a thousand years old, even if her face says she is only twenty!'

'Audouard, you speak as though you want to protect her from me. I promise you I have no ill intention. Do you know her well?'

'It is true that I admire the woman,' said the glazier, turning his face away. 'But you are a man of faith. I have found my blue, so why should not you also find what you seek with such ardour?'

He fell silent for a moment.

'By the way, Galeran,' he said, 'we are burying Jérôme today at the church of Saint André. The funeral procession will pass by Notre Dame so that his colleagues can escort him. It would be good if you were there. And, if you wish, I could introduce you to the master foreman.'

'You are right, Audouard. I shall indeed give your colleague a final salute. And I shall happily meet your master foreman and admire your work, which I am sure will be just as impressive as it was at Saint-Denis.'

*

Audouard presented Galeran to Thiberge de Soissons as soon as they arrived at Notre Dame.

The master foreman, who wore a brown smock and leather boots, was a giant of a man. Bald, broad-shouldered, his big hands gripping a cane, he seemed anchored to the ground. His bearded face, although a little chubby from culinary excess, was still handsome. But the most striking thing about him were the little black eyes that looked as though nothing would escape their attention.

'Good day to you, Sir,' he said in his boomnig voice. 'Audouard tells me you spent some time at Saint-Denis and that Abbé Suger counts you among his friends. Two very good reasons to welcome you here at Notre Dame! I dare say it is unnecessary to advise you to take care. You well know the dangers of this work and of the rigour required for our success. I own that I am particularly uncompromising. I feel responsible for my men, and yesterday's accident reinforces this feeling.'

'I understand your concern, Master. Such deaths are still far too numerous. I am told you have had the scaffolding strengthened and you now make those of your men who are most at risk rope themselves together. A wise decision, for I am sure that there must be strong winds on this hill.'

'Indeed. But the wind is just one of the dangers my men are faced with.'

At that moment an apprentice working nearby was cut in the face by a splinter of stone. The master foreman excused himself and hurried off to tend to the boy.

Audouard soon also went to rejoin his men, leaving Galeran to wander through the cathedral on his own.

17

The knight had a notion whose veracity he wished to confirm. For that he needed a fellow countryman, a Breton, for men would always speak more openly with their own kind.

He observed the tower, the scaffolding, the pulley systems. Then he talked to a mason, but did not get the answer he sought. He asked the same question of a stonecutter, and this time met with more success.

'There are some Bretons on the site. Quite a few, in fact. Carpenters, most of them. Look, there's one. He's a mason, that one, going up the ladder with the hod.'

Galeran saw a man with a hod that had two handles, which were placed one on either side of his head so that he could keep his hands free as he climbed.

Galeran watched the masons working the mortar with their trowels as he waited for the man to come back down again. The stonecutter told him that the Breton mason had been working in Chartres for ten years.

He finally climbed back down the ladder and the knight went to him. The man, whose stubborn face was lined like a piece of old wood, nodded his head as he listened to Galeran's questions. Then he responded rapidly in the guttural tongue of his land. Galeran asked further questions, but the old worker suddenly shook his head and retreated into an obstinate silence. Galeran took no offence, saluted the man amicably and went to sit on top of a pile of cut stones a little distance from the site.

From his perch he could see the wicker structures that served as a floor for the workers while they erected the cathedral's walls. The weather was fine, the workers above him sang at the tops of their voices, and he could hear the foreman barking out orders. The stonecutters' chisels cut into the rock, sending forth sharp splinters of stone. A heavy mallet fell from a walkway. At the other end of the site, two workers dumped their barrowful of bricks and a thick cloud of dust momentarily enveloped the sweating men.

Galeran pondered the fire that had ravaged the town eleven years before, and he wondered at the strange destiny that made a healer of Ausanne. Many said redheads were the daughters of the Devil and brought bad luck, but the knight had always been fascinated by their flaming hair and their milky skin.

Without knowing what sparked his train of thought, Galeran suddenly saw himself back on the field of battle, his sword stained with the blood of his enemies. He remembered his pride and his enthusiasm for war. He saw again the pits where bodies burned. Then the vision disappeared as quickly as it had begun, and Galeran, his calm restored, thought of the pitiful body of the old man by the banks of the Eure.

'Sir, *Sir*!' insisted a youthful voice.

Galeran looked down and recognised Benoît.

'Good day to you, little brother. Why do you honour me with your visit?'

'My sister told me to fetch you. She has gone to the Prévôté and cannot accompany me to the river.'

'And just why should Ausanne want me to go with you to the river?'

'I found the dead man's clothes, Sir, near Béguines.'

'Ah, now I see. I didn't think you'd just sit around and sulk. Well then, let us go and see what you have found. You can tell me how you came across them on the way.'

They passed alongside the walls of the Palais Comtal and began their descent to the river, chatting as they walked. The boy spoke excitedly of his discovery.

'This place, it's a bit of wasteland where we like to go, there's never many people about there. A good spot for fishing, you can catch trout and even dace. That's where I found the old man's clothes. At least, I think they're his clothes. After all, only madmen or the dead abandon their clothes.'

They arrived at the enclosure and took a path that led them through bramble and gorse bushes and then down a steep slope to the river. Benoît pointed to a pile of clothes near a rickety, moss-covered pier.

'I touched nothing,' said the boy.

'You did well,' said Galeran, bending down to examine the clothes. 'It looks like the Provost's men are not as talented as yourself, my young friend.'

'They're a pack of good-for-naughts!' said the boy scornfully. 'They've no more sense than a rabbit.'

'Let's see what we have here. Good quality breeches, a shirt, purple-coloured old boots . . . Very light clothing for an old man about to bathe on a rainy night. A man recovering from a fever, to boot. And he didn't take anything to dry himself with. A little unorthodox, I would say. Perhaps they want us to believe he was one of those madmen who bathe whatever the weather, summer or winter, who will even break the ice to have their swim!'

Galeran glanced at the surrounding bushes.

'What are you looking for, Sir?'

'I don't know, Benoît. Something unusual.'

'Look, there's something!' said Benoît, and he picked up two short lengths of rope that had lain hidden in the long grass.

'Put them with the clothes and let's have another look around,' said Galeran.

He thought he had seen something in the brambles. Drawing his sword, he cut through the undergrowth and from beneath a mulberry bush he took up a large hessian sack.

'Well, well, this may be yet another piece of evidence. But it all seems too easy. My friend, go and fetch the sergeant or a man-at-arms.'

'Yes, Sir,' said the boy, and off he ran.

Galeran sat down by the river and tried to imagine the events that had taken place here that rainy night. He picked up the pieces of rope and examined them.

'Strange; the murderer wanted it to look like an accident. The clothes were in a neat pile, and the rain washed away any footprints. Yet whoever it was left the rope and the sack that was most likely used to transport the body.'

He was inspecting the sack, scratching with his nail at a long, dark streak encrusted on the cloth, when Benoît returned with one of the Provost's men. Galeran got to his feet.

'This young man and I are both of the opinion that these

are the clothes you are looking for. Where can I find the Provost?'

'He is on his way, Sir. He would like you to wait for him.'

A breathless Provost soon arrived, with two more of his men in tow, at the steep slop that led down to the river.

'Decidedly, Sir, we were destined to meet again. You say you have found the old man's clothes?'

'It was Benoît, Ausanne's youngest brother, who discovered them.'

'Come here, boy. Don't be afraid,' said the Provost. 'Are you sure these are the man's clothes? You didn't touch anything?'

'No, Sir,' replied the boy, clearly intimidated by the Provost's booming voice and imposing figure. 'But I knew they were the jeweller's clothes, for I recognised his boots. They were a fine pair, and he wore them all the time.'

'You knew the man?'

'I saw him at my sister's when he had the fever.'

'We also found a cloth sack that was probably used to conceal the body,' said Galeran. 'Look at these stains, they look very like blood, do they not? And see these pieces of rope. There are knots in them, but it looks as if they were cut to save time.'

'By God, you are right, Chevalier Galeran! Now, you layabouts, search the whole area and find me something else!' roared the Provost, clearly furious that it was not his men who had discovered these clues. 'And we have not yet found the innkeeper and his wife. Their serving girl told us they were at La Hanterie. As you see, Galeran, you are well ahead of us!'

Galeran returned to the cathedral and sat near the forge to wait for Audouard.

'Have you been there all day?' asked the glazier when he arrived.

'No, I have had a rather busy day. But I'll tell you about it later. I have learned that in Chartres there is a Breton brotherhood, under the patronage of Saint-Malo.'

'That's right. We have here some fine carpenters from that part of the world. Actually, the brotherhood is quite powerful, and is respected as much by the Palais Comtal as it is by the chapter, which is rather exceptional. It recently had a shipment of stones from Berchères brought here to help with the reconstruction of Notre Dame.'

'The mason I spoke to today told me the brotherhood meets in a house on Rue de la Bretonnerie.'

'That I did not know. But I can show you where the street is.'

'Yes, please do, for I hope to put some questions to my countrymen. And how was your day?'

'We put the first part of my stained glass into its frame. I can take you to see it if you like. As you know, it is customary for us to celebrate as each stage of the glass is put in. So tonight we are going to Ambroise's inn. I hope you will join us.'

'With pleasure. It will be just like our drinking bouts in Saint-Denis!'

'Drinking bouts! I think you exaggerate. I don't think I have ever seen you drunk, despite the lively company we used to keep in that happy time!'

Audouard guided Galeran towards the scaffolding. The two men climbed nimbly up to where a piece of stained glass was being inserted into its frame.

Two large panels had already been placed in the metal fittings. Audouard took Galeran inside the building so that he could judge the quality of the stained glass with the light behind it.

The day was nearing its end, and a soft light illuminated the glass, spattering the men with blue.

Galeran, fascinated, stared at the first panels that were going to make up the Jesse tree. Then he turned to look at Audouard.

'"Light is the truth of the world",' murmured the knight. 'You have succeeded, Audouard. I have never seen such a blue, not even in Saint-Denis. How did you create it? I would think that such a colour could be achieved only by pulverising sapphires and melting them into the glass.'

'Abbé Suger did indeed grind many a sapphire to get his azure – which was another source of discord between him and Bernard de Clairvaux – but here, alas, we do not have the means that were at his disposal.'

'I once heard Suger say that a master glazier could be judged by his blue. I'm beginning to think he was right. When will the rest of the glass be put in? I hope it will be before I leave. But if not, I promise I shall return to admire it.'

Audouard took his friend's hands in his own.

'I know your words are sincere.'

'Yes, friend,' replied Galeran.

Then he stood back a little to have another look at the limpid, greenish-blue that Audouard had invented.

The pair climbed down to the ground, where they were soon joined by apprentice glaziers and other companions. The little group then headed off towards the Coeur Couronné rotisserie. After the customary courtesies, the workers began paying homage to their master. They each took it in turn to praise him, and libation followed libation. The glasswork had not yet been officially blessed, so the men offered it up to God and to Our Lady and beseeched them for their protection.

Galeran and Audouard drank with the apprentices for a while, then withdrew to their favourite table for a repast of delicious lamb roasted on a spit.

'I would like to hear a little more about the people who work with you,' said Galeran. 'You said most of them came from Saint-Denis like yourself. Can you think of someone whose reasons for coming here might be different to your own?'

'No, I cannot,' mumbled Audouard, taking his head in his hands.

'The old Breton told me today that a strange man was living in the cathedral, that he even spent his nights there. But he would not say his name. Perhaps you know it?'

'It is true that Enguerrand never leaves the cathedral. I know the man well enough. The master foreman is happy that he is there, for he keeps away the goliards and anyone else who might be tempted to sneak in at night and steal material. I did not speak of him to you, for he is a unique character. He has taken a vow to live as a recluse. He lives only for Our Lady. I met him at Saint-Denis, where he worked for several years and where he became a master of his trade.'

'Enguerrand . . . Do I know the man?'

'I think not. He is a master stonecutter, but he always works alone. Except for some very rare occasions, he will not tolerate the company of others. He does not even have an apprentice! Only Thiberge has any merit in his eyes, and he has contact with him for reasons of work only. He has no friends . . . But I find it hard to see him as a destroyer. Just the opposite, in fact. He has given himself entirely to the cathedral of Notre Dame. He is passionate about it. The master foreman appreciates his work, for he is an extraordinary artist. Every stone he touches comes to life, and his statues are like no other man's!'

'I must say that I find his life quite astonishing. And our valiant master foreman? Is there anything odd about him?'

'He, too, is a man beyond reproach, and he comes with the highest recommendations. But you have met him yourself and you know that the cathedral is all that matters to him.'

'Have they found the man who is supposed to be Jérôme's friend?'

'No, they still do not know who he is. The Provost believes his death was an accident. Perhaps he's right. I shall have another talk with Thiberge de Soissons tomorrow, and if he says anything new I shall let you know.'

'Tell me, Audouard, you said it rained the night before I arrived?'

'I did. Why do you ask?'

'I shall tell you in a moment. But first let me tell you about my afternoon. You know Ausanne's little brother, the little chap we met the other day? Well, he found the drowned man's clothes near the Eure. It would have been very unlikely that a man that age would go for a swim in bad weather, particularly if he didn't bring anything to dry himself with. Not only that, but we found a sack big enough to hold a man's body. And it had blood stains on it.'

'By God, the poor man was . . . '

'Murdered, Audouard. Murdered, and by someone who tried to make it look like an accident! But what I find hard to explain is that whoever it was left too many clues.'

The curfew was sounded. Ambroise, hurrying the last guests out, bade farewell to the two men.

'Here, sirs, take these torches and make haste. It is better not to linger in the streets, given what happened to that poor wretch down by the river. The men-at-arms are jumpy.'

They had gone but a short distance from the rotisserie when they came upon a patrol. The sergeant saluted them.

'Good evening, sirs. You are out late tonight.'

'Indeed. I am celebrating my friend's visit to our town.'

'Welcome to Chartres, Sir. But you must get home quickly. We have already put up the chains. Good night to you, gentlemen.'

The patrol marched away, and silence fell again. A stray dog ran up to them, seeking company for the night. Our friends hurried off towards Rue au Lait.

18

Night had fallen on the great cathedral. An icy north wind raged around Notre Dame, making the woodwork groan and buffeting the scaffolding. Grotesque shadows, cast by clouds flitting over the moon, fell across the statues on the portals.

A dull sound, like that of a hammer covered in a piece of cloth, was heard high up in the building, where a faint light could be glimpsed. The noise stopped and started, as though whoever laboured there sought to avoid detection.

In a nearby street, a figure standing in a doorway lit a torch. The man then moved towards the cathedral. He walked silently, stopping now and then, listening, moving on.

The noise high up in the building started again, as though the worker had found fresh resolve. The blows became more and more violent, and strange creaking noises could now be heard. Suddenly came the crash of breaking glass.

The man in the street began to run. The tiny light that played behind the stained-glass window was extinguished, and silence once again took hold of the site.

He finally stopped at the foot of the cathedral and held up his torch. A pile of debris lay at his feet, the torchlight picking out a thousand glittering specks. He fell, as though struck by an evil spell, to his knees and collapsed in a swoon.

19

Ausanne's thoughts were on the knight. The attraction she felt towards him had woken old sorrows that lay dormant in the depths of her soul. She could not sleep. She climbed out of bed, lit a candle and went to her workbench.

Taking a long knife, she sharpened it on a stone and began cutting up the bark of a silver willow. This was a sovereign remedy for rheumatism and fever, and she had promised to take some to an old friend of her mother's in the morning.

The blade cut forcefully into the bark. Ausanne worked quickly, and had soon filled a small clay jar with the bark strips. The light from the candle illuminated her tense face, revealing pursed lips and eyes half-closed in concentration.

A soft knock on the door made her jump. She held the knife behind her back and went stealthily to the door. She hesitated a moment before flinging it open.

But, as had happened every night for several months now, there was no one there. On the doorstep fluttered a few scarlet petals.

'Come back, whoever you are, come back!' cried the young woman.

She bent down to pick up a petal but then, alarmed at her own imprudence, pushed the door shut and drew across the heavy bar.

Her hand pressed against her breast to calm her thumping heart, she took up her candle and returned to bed. These nocturnal visits and mysterious offerings worried her. She had not yet managed to spy anyone or anything in the dark lane. All she ever heard was a quiet panting, almost like a groan, that sometimes preceded the scratching on the oak door.

Ausanne slid the knife under her pillow and blew out the candle. Sleep took her, and the petal crumpled in her hand.

A bud appears on the tree of Jesse,
A shoot grows out of its roots.
Its word is the staff that beats those that are violent,
The breath from its lips kills the wicked.
Justice is the cloth that covers its loins,
Loyalty the sash around its waist . . .

No, Lord, Your staff has not touched me,
No, I am not dead, not yet,
For I have drunk the wine of my anger . . .
Oh, Mother! Take pity on your son
I shall destroy all that evokes your death . . .
He has imprisoned the blue of the sky
In the liquid of his glass . . .
I shall free it from the stone,
This blue shall never be given unto men . . .
Never!

PART THREE

If thou know not . . . Go thy way forth.

Solomon 1, 8

20

The Rovin Vignon inn had two floors and was thus a little higher than the surrounding houses. On the ground floor was a dining area, a large back room and a kitchen. A trap door led into the cellar where barrels of wine were stored. The innkeeper's bedchamber took up most of the upper floor. A staircase as steep as a ladder led up to two attic rooms and a communal room reserved for pilgrims and the less wealthy travellers.

The morning Angelus had not yet been rung but La Doëtte was already sweeping up, brushing the debris of the previous night into the fireplace. When she had done with the cleaning she took armfuls of thyme and sage from a large wicker basket and scattered them across the clay floor.

Hearing a noise upstairs, she rushed back to the hearth to stir up the embers and throw a bundle of firewood under the heavy cauldron full of water that hung in the hearth.

She gave a little sigh of relief when she saw the twigs flare up. Now she had only to go to the pantry, fetch a cob loaf of black bread, some dried sausage, and some goat's cheese and set it all out on a long table near the door.

La Doëtte was fourteen years old but looked no more than ten. She was like a small worried animal, afflicted by a perpetual trembling. Fatigue and fear already marked her grubby face, and dark rings hung beneath her eyes.

Two months previously she had thought she was going to die, and this on account of an old clay pot she dropped. Her mistress fell upon her, a rush in her hand, grabbed her by the hair and dragged her to the cellar. There, despite the girl's cries and pleas, she whipped her until her arm was too tired to go on.

The innkeeper, going to the cellar to fill a jug from the barrel, found La Doëtte unconscious and covered in blood and vomit. He wrapped her in an old pelisse and brought her to Ausanne's house on Rue Percheronne.

The physician was not taken in by the man's embarrassed explanations. When she had washed the bruised little body, she turned to the innkeeper and stared at him indignantly.

'Master Jehan, you and your wife have the right to punish your servant, but you do not have the right to kill her! If ever you beat her like this again, I shall be obliged to inform the Provost. Now leave me!'

Dame Ausanne kept the little one with her for four days until her fever abated.

'Four fine days,' mused La Doëtte, 'four days in Heaven.'

And after four days she returned to Hell.

The innkeeper's wife did stop beating La Doëtte after Ausanne's warning, but the girl remained on her guard and avoided being alone with her employer. She had been at the Rovin Vignon for just three months, but already she understood why so many servants had come and gone before her. At first she had naïvely thought they had not been doing their work properly. But the blows and humiliations her mistress rained down upon her soon told La Doëtte that the woman's wicked moods were the sole cause of her predecessors' early departure.

La Doëtte herself often thought about leaving, but she badly needed the work. Her ageing mother was ill, and the few sous the girl earned enabled her to bring her bread and vegetables each day, and even, on a good day, some bacon or sausage.

'Doëtte,' called the innkeeper, 'your mistress wants some water to wash herself. Bring her some. Quickly. Have you made my breakfast yet?'

'Yes, Master. It's ready. I'll take the water up now.'

The girl poured some water into a large pitcher and took it upstairs. She knocked on her mistress's door.

'Come in,' said a soft voice.

'Good day, Mistress,' said La Doëtte, as she went towards the bed strewn with pelisses on which Mahaut lay. 'I have brought you some warm water.'

The woman's pale, naked breasts contrasted with the bright red of the cushions that surrounded her.

'Have you fetched my ointment?'

'Yes, Mistress. Here it is.'

La Doëtte took from her purse a little clay pot sealed with wax. It contained a mixture of oils extracted from rosemary, juniper, savory and lemon balm. The woman seized it, flicked off the cork and sniffed it with delight.

'So, tell me,' she said.

'Yes, Mistress. I went to Vieux Fossés yesterday evening before I went to see Mother. The old woman wasn't sitting out in front of her shack as usual and I was afraid to go in so I waited by the willow tree. Then she arrived in an old barge that she hid in the long grass.'

'I know, Doëtte. I know all that already. Go on.'

'But you don't know how much she frightens me, that woman! I threw the purse at her so I wouldn't have to touch her. She went inside to get your pot like she always does. Then she put it on her doorstep and went back in and locked the door. And that's all. I ran off because it was already getting dark and it's a long way to my mother's.'

As she spoke, she poured the water into a basin on the mat that covered the floor. Then she fetched a long, white, linen shirt for her mistress.

Mahaut decided it was time to get out of bed. She pulled aside the sheets and the wadded covers to reveal a white, carefully depilated body.

She was a woman who seemed both cunning and guileless. Her limbs were slender, her breasts small and firm, and her hips broad. With her straight little nose and slightly protruding eyes, she looked a little like the statue of Eve that Gislebertus sculpted on the great door of the cathedral of Saint-Lazare d'Autun.

As in a ritual she had carried out a thousand times before, she climbed off the bed and stood with her feet in the middle of the basin La Doëtte had filled with warm water. The serving girl took the perfumed oil the old woman had given her and began rubbing it over her mistress's body. The innkeeper's wife stretched out like a cat under the fingers that massaged her neck and back, her breasts and her little round stomach.

La Doëtte then wet a cloth, washed her mistress's face and poured the rest of the water over her perfumed body. Mahaut stepped out of the basin and let the girl vigorously dry her off.

She slipped over her head the white shirt the servant handed her, sat down on the edge of the bed and began undoing her long plaits. La Doëtte sat behind her and with a comb slowly brushed the long, thick, brown hair.

'That's enough! Leave me,' cried Mahaut, suddenly nervous, pushing the girl away. 'And tell my husband to come up and see me.'

The innkeeper, informed of his wife's wishes, gulped down the rest of his breakfast and hurried upstairs.

'How beautiful you are, Mahaut,' he said as he stood at the end of the bed, his eyes shining. 'What may I do for you?'

'Get rid of that girl! I detest her! I hate her false modesty and the way she looks at you.'

Mahaut's voice was soft, but her tone showed she would countenance no argument.

'She works hard, you know. She's the best servant we've had,' pleaded the innkeeper.

'I'm fed up. I don't trust her any more. She'll end up spreading rumours about us just like all the others.'

'Why should she? Even if she doesn't like us, she has no interest in harming us. She needs the money we pay her to feed her mother. You know that.'

'Jehan, do you wish to vex me?'

He looked at the round breasts that lay exposed by her unfastened shirt and placed his fat hand on her shoulder.

'No,' he answered, his voice hoarse. 'Never, by God, would I seek to displease you.'

The woman smiled, revealing two rows of little teeth that were very white and very sharp.

'I love you,' she said, putting her arm around his powerful neck.

He suddenly brushed her hand aside, lifted her up by the waist and threw her onto the bed. He pulled off her shirt, spread her long, white legs and lay down on her, seeking his pleasure. Mahaut groaned as he brutally penetrated her. A fine layer of sweat covered her temples, her eyes fixed coldly on the ceiling.

21

Galeran left Audouard's early that morning to seek out Ausanne's house. He asked two or three passers-by and was soon on the right track. Everyone in Chartres seemed to know where the young physician lived.

It was a little wooden house on Rue Percheronne, within the cloister of Notre Dame, facing onto the walls of the new Hôtel-Dieu. Here the young woman lived and, when she was not out on visits, received her many patients. On both sides of the house was a pretty kitchen garden, bordered by a fence made of rushes woven together. Two gnarled old apple trees stood in the midst of a profusion of vegetables, flowers and herbs, sheltering under their branches a brood of turtledoves.

The shutter of the building's only window lay open to let in the sun. A large white cat sat on the sill, diligently cleaning itself. Galeran gave three light knocks on the ancient door. The call brought Ausanne to the window, where she leaned on her elbows to stroke the cat.

'Good day, Sir. What a surprise to see you here. Are you perhaps suffering from insomnia or some other complaint?'

'Good day,' said Galeran, whose face brightened so much at the sight of Ausanne that she had to smile. 'I like to rise early, and even more so if I know I will be seeing you! I am not ill, but if I were you would be a most welcome replacement for my last doctor, a toothless old man who smelled more of cheap wine than of medicine!'

'Oh, Chevalier Galeran, let us stay on more solid ground. I am not a woman for idle banter. What can I do for you? And tell me, how is it that a stranger to the town can find my lodgings so early in the morning?' she asked, her pretty eyes fixed on the knight's.

'Madam, you are renowned in this town. One has only to ask in the street. Please do not be offended that I have sought you out so early. May I come in? I would like to talk to you about that poor old man's death.'

Ausanne hesitated a moment, then gave a half-smile.

'Very well, Sir. I accept the terms of your truce. One moment.'

The knight heard a bolt being drawn back.

'Audouard said people here leave their doors open at night,' he said as Ausanne pushed open the door.

'They do. And I usually do too,' replied Ausanne.

The knight's question had made her feel ill at ease. She stood aside to let him enter the house. There was but one room which served as her workplace by day and her bedroom by night. Through a little door at the back a courtyard could be seen in which there was an oven and a shed that housed the latrines and the tubs and basins used for washing. Thyme, verbena and sage were strewn across the earth floor. Their powerful aroma mingled with the smell of crushed leaves, bark and wild flowers.

But the most surprising thing was the explosion of vibrant colour on the ceiling that formed a sort of living canopy over the room. From each beam hung bouquets of dried plants, each a distinct hue. The arnica and the greater celandine were yellow, the carthamus orange, the flax, chicory and cornflower blue, the foxglove purple, and the hyssop and mallow a dark shade of purple.

In the middle of the room stood a long table on which sat a collection of small dishes, pots and bowls. A jar held fine strips of bark. At the other end of the table was a sieve filled with Saint John's wort picked before dawn that very morning and still wet with dew. A set of scales jangled above the work area and a large stone mortar stood in a corner.

Two long benches and some folding stools provided seating next to a small brazier, mounted on wheels, which served both to heat the room and for the preparation of remedies.

On a workbench along the wall was a writing case where each evening Ausanne would record her observations. Dozens of neatly stacked rolls of vellum filled her shelves. The young woman had installed her bed in the farthermost corner of the room, behind a curtain. The narrow cot had a checked cover and stood between the fireplace and a large chest. On a credence table stood three objects – a silver ewer, a little casket inlaid with ivory, and a pretty pewter mirror – whose elegance contrasted with the simplicity of the room.

'I see you have noticed my credence. Beautiful, is it not? A rich patient wanted to pay me a large amount of money for my services, but I refused. So he gave me these things instead.'

She held out a wooden bowl.

'A present from another patient. But this one had no money to pay me.'

Made from the wood of a fruit tree, the bowl had carved on its side a strange animal that seemed to coil itself around the vessel. It had the head of a bird of prey, the breasts of a woman and the body of a dragon whose wings were spread for flight.

'Very fine work, and very unusual,' said Galeran. 'As is your house. And you yourself, I might add. May I ask what you write on the parchment?'

'Observations about my patients, and the recipes for my remedies. But you wished to speak to me about something?' said Ausanne, who appeared not to want to let the conversation become too personal.

Galeran put down the wooden bowl and stepped back a little.

'Forgive me. I had forgotten the reason for my visit. I believe you know the innkeepers from Rue Fulbert?'

'I have met them. I treated their servant La Doëtte.'

'She was ill?'

'No! The innkeeper brought her to me unconscious and covered in blood. Her mistress had beaten her so badly that she nearly died. The poor thing's not the strongest of children, and she was whipped at least twenty times. I told the innkeeper I would report him to the Provost if it happened again. I kept the girl with me for four days, for I feared for her life. But they seem to have been behaving themselves since.'

'Why did they whip the child?'

'La Doëtte said it was merely on account of some clumsiness. I think it was a plate she dropped. By God, but I hate that Mahaut hussy!' exclaimed the physician, her voice full of contempt.

'Calm yourself, Dame Ausanne! We could still mention the affair to the Provost if we dine with him. But who could tell me more about the innkeepers? Are they from this region?'

'No. No one here knows them very well. They arrived just a short time ago and the only company they keep is their own. But they were quickly accepted into the guild, they pay their taxes, and they hear mass regularly. He is called Jehan de Toulouse and her name is Mahaut. La Doëtte says Dame Mahaut does little but buy perfumes and ointments and sits in her room all day waiting for her husband. The man must have a small fortune put away. It's not with his earnings from the inn that he can afford to pamper his wife like he does. It was a year ago that Jehan bought the inn. The man he bought it from, who hails from Chartres, said he did not even haggle about the price! As for Mahaut, although she always dresses like a grand lady and never shows her face to anyone, some say she is really the daughter of the old woman by the river who has come back to her home town.'

'The old woman by the river?'

'Yes. An odd story. Sit down, Sir, and please excuse my nerves. I slept poorly last night,' said Ausanne, holding a stool out to Galeran. 'The old woman is a strange character, perhaps something of a witch, who lives near Vieux Fossés.'

'Vieux Fossés?'

'A long time ago the people of Chartres diverted the Eure so as to irrigate their crops. The place between the two branches of the river became known as Vieux Fossés. The woman lives there in a shack by the riverbank. She takes great pleasure in frightening everyone, but she's not a bad woman. She has the hands of a healer and there is no one to match her for resetting a dislocated shoulder. But whether or not she can cause death as easily as she gives life, I cannot say. Some believe she can. There is no one better for finding plants that grow by the river, and sometimes I ask her to find me teasel, sundew or *consoude*.

'Some say that a long time ago, she was so beautiful that a lord from Blois fell in love with her and that she bore him a bastard child. The child was so pretty that the lord took her with him to his château. The gossips say he was so lovestruck he would have brought the mother too, if she had so desired. But a few years later he returned to Chartres and brought the girl with him. It appears he threw the girl from his horse in front of the shack and galloped off. Three years passed, during which the girl lived like a wild animal, before it was the mother's turn to chase her away. No one knew why and no one has ever seen her since.'

'Strange that neither mother nor father wanted to keep her. And why do they think this Mahaut is the old woman's daughter?'

'Those who knew the child say Mahaut resembles her. But she was only ten years old when she left. La Doëtte told me her mistress often sends her to get ointments from the old woman, but there is nothing strange in that. The people of Chartres may not be fond of her, but they appreciate that she knows her herbs and makes the best ointments. But what is strange is that Mahaut apparently makes La Doëtte describe each visit in detail, and that the innkeeper's wife seems to be familiar with the place despite the fact that she never leaves the upper town.'

'Very interesting. Ausanne, can you help me? Come with me to the inn. I want to ask La Doëtte a few questions before the Provost gets to her and frightens her with his boorish manners.'

'What do you want to ask her?'

'First I would like to find out a little more about the charming couple who run the establishment. Secondly, by all accounts it seems that when the dead man disappeared, so did his entire stock of precious stones. I would like to know where they went. And I have a question for you, too, if you would be so kind as to answer it. You say you treated the dead man. Was that the first time you met him?'

'Yes . . . Well, no. It was the first time he had come to me for medicine, but I had the impression that I had seen him somewhere before. But La Doëtte will certainly know more about him than I do.'

'Do you know his name?'

'He told me but I forget. All I remember is that he came

from Champagne. Now, are we finished with your questions or should I give up all hope of doing any work today?' asked Ausanne, a note of impatience in her voice.

'One last question, if you please,' replied Galeran, who appeared not to have noticed her change of humour. 'What conclusion did you come to after you examined the body? Did you change your mind about the cause of death?'

'No. I am still convinced the man was murdered. His skull was smashed, and given the state of the body, I would say he died as early as Sunday night.'

'You know, Ausanne, I have rarely seen someone so young so sure of herself. You are more rigorous and sharp-witted than many physicians who have been in the trade for decades.'

'Please refrain from paying me compliments I do not deserve. When you live near a river you frequently come across drowned bodies. Mostly they are accidents, but sometimes we fish out people who have taken their own lives. And furthermore, I am no longer so young, and I have been a physician for some time now. Sir, I do not wish to chase you from my home, but it is getting late and I have many visits to make. If we are to go and see La Doëtte, then let us do so without further ado.'

Paying no more attention to the knight, she took her bag and a wicker basket and opened the door. Galeran followed silently behind her.

22

The innkeeper and his wife had gone out, summoned by the Provost. They had left their serving girl to look after the Rovin Vignon's rare morning customers.

'Good day to you, La Doëtte,' said Ausanne, kissing the girl on both cheeks and handing her the wicker basket. 'Here, this is for you and your mother. Some of the herbs and tisanes you like. How are you?'

'I am fine, thank you, miss. But you spoil me! Mother and I pray for you every day to Our Lady.'

'Are you here on your own?'

'Yes. Sergeant Geoffroy came to take Jehan and Mahaut to see the Provost. About old Ogier. And our only two guests, the jeweller's apprentices, have gone out too.'

'This is Galeran de Lesneven,' said Ausanne. 'He's a visitor to Chartres. He would like to ask you a few questions.'

'Very well, Dame Ausanne,' said the girl, lowering her eyes.

'Doëtte, you said the man's name was Ogier?' the knight asked softly.

'Yes, Sir. Ogier de Reims, that is what they called him.'

'Have the Provost's men already visited Ogier's room?'

'No, Sir. Not that I know of.'

'Doëtte, can I ask a favour of you? Will you take me to his room? I want to see if we can find some sort of clue there.'

'I'm not sure I should,' said the girl, with a questioning look at Ausanne.

'Do not be afraid,' said the physician. 'I shall keep watch while you two go up. That way you won't be caught out if your master returns.'

La Doëtte blushed and agreed. She led Galeran upstairs to a door that opened onto a tidy little bedroom in the attic.

A ray of sunshine filtered in through an open shutter. Apart from a bed covered in pelisses, the only furniture in the room was a chest filled with clothes upon which rested a washbasin. A traveller's cloak and an old leather bag hung on a nail.

'Old Ogier never went out without his cloak,' said the servant, pointing to the garment. 'Come rain or shine, he always had it on. It was a present from his late wife, and very dear to him.'

Galeran nodded and went to the window, where he pulled the shutters wide open. The wind whistled into the room. Directly in front of the window, the cathedral rose majestically towards the sky.

From the jeweller's room the entire site was visible. Galeran had not realised just how close the inn was to Notre Dame. He thought he could make out the figure of his friend Audouard busy at the foot of the building.

He looked out for quite a while, thinking about Jérôme's fall, which had taken place directly in front of where he now stood, and of Ogier's death. Then he began searching the room. Finding nothing in the chest, he looked under the straw mattress and the cushions, but again drew a blank. He took the leather bag and looked for the jeweller's precious stones there. But he found only toiletries, a seal with the initials O. R., a pair of tweezers and a small set of scales.

'Doëtte, did you know the old man well? Had he stayed here before?'

'I have been here only these past three months, but I was told he came here every year before the May holy days. He was friends with the last owner of the inn, that's why he came back. I think he has some clients in the Bishop's palace and in the Palais Comtal.'

'How do you know that?'

'He liked to chat, especially with the mistress. Sometimes I overheard them,' said the girl, a little embarrassed, by way of excuse.

'Did he ever show you his jewels?'

'Of course. He was not a modest man. He showed me them almost every morning. Most were blue, and he had some red ones, and he had some with a complicated name that changed colour. Ice blue stones, he called them.'

'Now, think hard. Had he sold his gems before he disappeared? Try to remember, it is important.'

'I know I saw them on Sunday. His pouch was on the bed when I brought him some water.'

'He didn't take it with him when he went out?'

'No, not always, Sir,' answered the girl, blushing again. 'The door to his room can be locked.'

'What did the pouch look like, Doëtte?'

'It was made of dark, red leather, with a black string.'

A sudden call from Ausanne made them rush out of the room and back down the stairs.

When the innkeeper and his wife walked back into their premises, they saw the serving girl pouring out wine for Galeran and Ausanne. Although surprised to see Ausanne in the company of a man, Jehan said nothing, simply nodding at the couple before joining Mahaut in her room. He looked worried.

Ausanne had reluctantly agreed to drink with the knight in order to make their presence seem a little less odd. Galeran ordered wine from the Loire. La Doëtte served them and then went outside to clean the tables and benches in front of the inn.

'To you, Dame Ausanne, and to the fine profession you practise with such skill,' said Galeran, raising his cup.

'And to you, Sir. May God protect you from all evil and may Our Lady watch over you.'

The young couple drank their wine with gravity. The knight's eyes left his companion only when a customer came into the inn.

'Strange, this cloak business,' he said.

'Which cloak?'

'The jeweller never went out without the cloak his late wife gave him, yet the cloak is still in his room.'

'So, this time he didn't take it with him. Or else . . . '

'Or else he was killed here!'

'You mean . . . ?'

'I don't mean anything. I do not yet possess enough facts to come to any conclusions,' said the knight, his brow furrowed. 'Unless the jeweller had sold the stones sometime on Sunday, whoever killed him made a pretty penny from their foul deed.

But why cover up the crime so badly? Why take his clothes and leave behind the cloak? I cannot understand this strange mix of precaution and blunder. And what does it all have to do with events at the cathedral?'

'What events at the cathedral?'

'A man has been killed on the site, and, according to my friend Audouard, there have been a lot of accidents in recent months.'

'A man killed? I haven't heard of this. When?'

'Monday evening.'

'I must have been at the leprosarium when it happened. I was there all day.'

'Not all day, for it was the day we met for the first time!'

Then, without paying any more attention to her words, the knight continued.

'The old man's life was connected to the cathedral in two ways. The first was his room.'

'His room?' said Ausanne.

'Did he see something he was not meant to see? Very possibly, given the position of his room. Secondly, the man had dealings with the Bishop's palace, for he sold diamonds there. Which of these two paths is the right one? Or was it merely his wealth that cost him his life? Forgive me, Dame Ausanne, I am thinking out loud, and I must be very poor company for you.'

'On the contrary, Sir. I find it fascinating. You are a strange fellow. I heard you tell the Provost your grandfather was a crusader. My great-uncle also went with his wife and two children to the kingdom of Jerusalem. Alas, we have since had no news of them. They left my father in charge of their house and garden. That's where I live now – my family gave it to me when I became a physician. At night I often dream that the four of them will return and come knocking at the door.'

'I think we most of us have relatives who have known the Holy Land. My grandfather, Florent de Lesneven, was thirty-eight years old when he joined the First Crusade inaugurated by Urban II. My father, Gilduin, was only five at the time, and my grandmother – and a fine, strong woman she was – was left alone to look after both him and the land. Like many others, she got into debt to keep up with the great expenses incurred by her husband. But my grandmother respected her spouse despite these difficulties, and would often tell me what a valiant knight he was. From the age of fifteen, my father took responsibility for the family. Our château was falling into ruin, and he worked tirelessly to repair it. He used the trowel and the ploughshare more often than the sword. My mother, who hailed from Gascony, brought as her dowry all the gaiety and insouciance of her origins. Today our family is a little less poor than it was, and my dear parents are still alive. I can only thank God for having given me such a courageous father and such a good mother.'

'Forgive me, knight, I did not mean to make you speak of so intimate a subject,' said Ausanne, intrigued by the sadness that had descended on Galeran's face.

'It is melancholy you see on my face, Dame Ausanne, not sadness. It is true that I do not like to speak of my family, but sometimes one memory awakens another. But let us speak of you, of your own childhood,' said Galeran, as he dreamily watched the light playing on the young woman's red curls.

'All I can say is that I had a happy childhood in an honest family of weavers. My mother, who is from Puiset, is a woman devoted to her family, and a hard taskmaster to boot. My father is strict but just. My sister Éloïse is a sweet girl and her beauty is matched only by her talent at weaving. Even the Bishop has recognised her skill and has commissioned a large tapestry of Notre Dame. And as for Benoît, you have met him already. He's as crafty as they come, and he knows more about fishing and hunting than he does about thread and needles!'

'But you have said nothing of yourself, Dame Ausanne. How is it that a weaver's daughter can be so bold as to become a physician?'

'And why not, Sir? I find you very keen to find out about my life! You should know that I do not like to speak of myself, especially to someone with whom I have been acquainted for a mere two days.'

Suddenly on the defensive, she had raised her voice a little, but now fell silent, surprised at the strength of her own words.

Galeran looked her in the eye before softly replying.

'Do not be mistaken, Dame Ausanne, and do not confuse me with somebody else. If I seek to know you better, it is because you hold me captive. Since our first meeting, your face has been ever present in my mind's eye. I respect you and admire the strength within you, even if, for the moment, I know not from where it comes. Do not be so secretive, open yourself a little to me. I wish you only well. And I am ready to swear before God that you shall not regret it.'

The knight had accompanied this last statement with so piercing a look that Ausanne coloured and looked away. She opened her mouth as though to reply, but then stood up and walked quickly out of the inn.

Galeran did not move for a moment, tight-lipped, not knowing how to react. Then he, too, stood up and ran after Ausanne to ask her to explain herself or, perhaps, to ask her forgiveness for his frankness. He jostled several customers as he rushed out of the inn, and they cursed him. But the knight's grave face and his sword dissuaded them from picking a fight. When he got to the street Ausanne was nowhere to be seen. He thought there would be little point in going to her home on Rue Percheronne as she would probably have gone to visit patients. And besides, even if she was there, she probably would not give him a warm welcome.

Seconds after Galeran left, the innkeeper rushed downstairs, buttoning up his breeches as he went. He was looking for La Doëtte, and spotted her outside serving a group of workers sitting around a table in the sunshine.

'Leave that and go up to see your mistress,' he said gently. 'She wants a word.'

The girl did as she was told. She trembled as she walked into the bedroom to find Mahaut standing in front of the open window, looking at the animals in the yard below. The mistress spoke to her servant without turning around.

'I think you have something to tell me, Doëtte.'

The terror the woman inspired in the girl suddenly overwhelmed her and she burst into tears.

'Oh, please! Enough!' Mahaut said brutally.

La Doëtte wiped her eyes with her sleeve. She was shaking all over.

'Good. That's better,' her mistress said dryly. 'Now you are going to tell me what your good friend Ausanne and her companion were doing here. Who was the man?'

'I do not know, Mistress. A knight . . . '

'I could see that. What was his name?'

'I heard Dame Ausanne call him Chevalier Galeran.'

La Doëtte lowered her eyes and blushed as she murmured: 'I think he is smitten with her.'

'What? He's fallen for that bitch?'

The girl nodded her head.

'Yes, he spoke soft words to her.'

Mahaut looked at her suspiciously.

'I hope for your sake you're telling me the truth,' she said, before adding gruffly, 'Tonight you can take what's left of the salt beef to your mother. Now go away, you vex me!'

La Doëtte, both amazed that she had got off so lightly and surprised at such generosity, left the room as though in a dream.

23

Galeran had reluctantly given up looking for Ausanne and was walking back towards the stables at Coeur Couronné to fetch his horse.

It was a bad day to be in Place de l'Étape au Vin. The square, known to locals as the 'Haunted Place', was cluttered with carts delivering oak planks. For here was sold not only wine but also the wood used to make barrels. The place was noisy at the best of times, but now it resounded with the cries of the carters exchanging jeers and broadsides.

It had all begun with one cart refusing to let another pass, and now the square was a complicated mass of carts and horses that blocked all movement and jammed the adjoining streets. Nobody wanted to yield to anyone else, and the criers from the various inns, well used to raising their voices, had joined in, shouting out in defence of the carts that were trying to deliver supplies to their taverns. A few mischievous passers-by were also sticking their oar in, defending whichever champions took their fancy.

A group of sturdy washerwomen set about an innkeeper whose cart was blocking their way. The unfortunate, a man not in the best of health, tried in vain to extricate himself from the gaggle of heckling creatures.

Galeran, although well used to Paris and the great Byzantine cities, had never seen such commotion. As he looked over the crowd he spotted the crier from the Coeur Couronné. Ambroise was in the middle of a tirade in which he boldly mixed wine, women and the plump bottom of a rival deivery man.

'A fine brawl, Sir,' he said when the knight walked up to him. 'Look at those women badgering that poor innkeeper, they'll be tearing the shirt off his back in a minute. It'll all turn sour if the Provost's men don't come very soon.'

His face red and sweating with excitement, Ambroise was clearly in his element.

'I own,' said the knight, 'that I have rarely seen such turbulence. Ambroise, I need my horse. You must aid me, for only a local man like yourself could get Quolibet out of your stables on a day like this.'

'Have no worry, Sir, I shall fetch him. Take Rue de la Fromagerie and wait for me in Place des Halles.'

Ambroise turned and walked off towards the stables, clearing a path for himself with a well-placed kick here or a shove there.

The knight went to the square and was about to sit down on a stone block when he saw a stable boy approach with Quolibet in tow. The horse was already saddled and its shining coat bore witness to the care it had received. Galeran tossed the boy a coin. He stroked his old companion's neck, then led him down through backstreets towards the Eure, carefully avoiding Place de l'Étape au Vin.

Porte Morard was never as busy as Porte Drouaise. A large crowd of travellers from Paris or Dreux might be clamouring at the latter, while the former would see only a handful of pilgrims, peasants or people going to the leprosarium at Grand-Beaulieu. Even the road here looked more like a bridle path than a highway. The poor state of the palisade symbolised the tollgate's lack of custom. Galeran heard a snore as he walked past the guard post, and smiled when he saw the guard slumped on the ground, his hood pulled down over his eyes. The knight mounted Quolibet and trotted off. The sun was high in the sky. Galeran took a deep breath, happy to be away at last from the din of the town.

He nodded a greeting to a group of pilgrims walking towards the tollgate and singing hymns as they went. He let the bridle hang down around his horse's neck. Quolibet, well used to his master's humours, sensed his melancholy and maintained a regular trot.

By the side of the road, two birds of prey tore into the remains of a young rabbit they had killed as it ventured out of its burrow.

'There are facts,' mused the knight, 'and there are lies and illusions. And at the end, if God wills it, there is the simple truth.'

He gazed at a flock of sheep that grazed among blossoming thorn bushes on the vast moor to his right.

What did he know? Not much. There was the building work at the cathedral and the death of Jérôme. And, opposite the cathedral, there was the inn with the beautiful Mahaut, who never let herself be seen without a veil, and there was the frightened little serving girl whose lies probably came as easily as her breath. There was the old jeweller they found in the river and his odd acolytes. But there was also Audouard, his friend, whose frankness seemed to have vanished along with his usual robust humour. And there was Ausanne, with her lovely pale complexion, inscrutable face and severe clothes.

Galeran suddenly spurred on his horse to a gallop. Some peasants crossed themselves as they watched him pass in a cloud of dust. Behind some trees he could see the hooded silhouette of a leper guiding a pair of oxen. A little further on he saw the high fence of the sanatorium, the little steeple of a modest chapel rising above it. Galeran slowed Quolibet down to a walk. Monks were coming and going along the road, accompanied by lepers, recognisable by their black cloaks.

Founded in 1054 by Comte Thibaud III on the right bank of the Eure, the Madeleine hospital had, due to an ever increasing number of patients, become the Grand-Beaulieu leprosarium. Run by monks, it received nobles, bourgeois and peasants suffering from leprosy or any other maladies of the skin which involved suppuration or which left marks whose cause could not be determined.

Galeran left the road and took the path leading to the sanatorium. Those lepers who were able to worked alongside the monks. Those more disabled kept to their beds, or sometimes walked around, dragging their limbs and occasionally shaking their rattles.

The people here rarely saw strangers and stared at Galeran as he dismounted and walked towards the entrance. A monk came and blocked his path.

'What is it you seek, Sir? This is a leprosarium. Have you a relative here?'

'No, brother. I have come to speak with your physician. I am a friend of Dame Ausanne of Chartres.'

'Ah!' said the monk, his face lighting up at the sound of the young woman's name. 'Come in. I shall take you to Frère Gacé. How has the dear lady been since she last came to see us?'

'When was that?'

'Monday, I think. Why do you ask? Ah, there's Gacé! Hey! Gacé!'

A monk, who had been striding through the enclosure with his habit billowing around his thick calves, turned to face them. His face horribly scarred, his hair dishevelled and his eyes sunk beneath bushy brows, Gacé had the air of a man who did not waste time in idle chatter.

Galeran stated the purpose of his visit.

'May the Lord shield you, brother. I am a friend of Dame Ausanne, and I need your help.'

The monk stared at him for a moment before replying.

'What do you want?'

'My question may seem strange, but I wish to know at what time Dame Ausanne left you on Monday.'

'Neither your own nor Dame Ausanne's affairs are of any interest to me. She left after Vespers, which was a little later than usual.'

Anger blazed in his eyes as he looked at Galeran.

'Dame Ausanne is a good woman,' he said. 'Do not believe anything to the contrary, no matter who is saying it.'

With these words, Gacé turned on his heels and marched off. Galeran wondered how the man had guessed at the doubts that plagued him.

24

The knight returned from his trip no less unsatisfied. He left his steed at the stables and went to the Rovin Vignon to see if he could find the jeweller's two aides. The pair were in the back room, sitting silently over a jug of wine. They gave a start when Galeran took a stool and sat down next to them.

'Oh, please be calm, sirs! How nervous you are, and what sad faces! Is it the Provost's company that made you like that? But I have not yet introduced myself. My name is Galeran de Lesneven and I have a few questions to put to you.'

'Why would a knight like you want to speak to us?' the older of the pair replied aggressively. 'We have nothing to say.'

The one with the stutter held his tongue.

'On the contrary, my good sirs,' said Galeran. 'I think you have quite a lot to say to me. And, by my faith, I shall not leave until you say it.'

The expression on his face told the men they had better give some ground.

'The Provost is not, as you know, the most gentle of men. He has worn us out,' groaned the older one, pressing his hand to his swollen chin. 'What do you want to know that he hasn't already asked?'

'I want to know the names of the people your master came here to see, and I want to know about the precious stones he was selling.'

'And just why should we tell you?' the man answered insolently.

'Because in principle I am much gentler than the Provost. Although in my part of the world, in Léon, people say it is better to have me as a friend than as a foe. They began saying this after I chopped a man in two with a single blow of my axe. Now, if you please, let the three of us talk frankly. If not . . . '

'No, no, that's fine. Our master was called Ogier de Reims.'

'That I know already. What sort of stones was he selling?'

'Garnets, sapphires, and some odd-looking stones that came from Hungary. Opals, he called them. He was the only one who sold them. They say that even Queen Aliénor had bought some from him.'

'Very good. And who were your clients here?'

'That we don't really know. Goldsmiths, people from the Palais Comtal and from the Bishop's palace. The master only needed us for the markets and to protect him while he was on the road. The rest of the time we did as we pleased while he conducted his affairs.'

'It seems you weren't exactly efficient at protecting him, my lambs.'

'We thought we were safe in Chartres. We've been coming here for years and there has never been any trouble.'

'Do you know the innkeepers?'

'No. They are new here. The wife is very beautiful. As for him, he's a touchy one. You wouldn't want to let him catch you looking sideways at his woman. But she liked old Ogier. They used to chat a lot, and she would lead him on. Just think! At his age.'

'And her husband said nothing?'

'Well, no. Given the poor state our master was in, there wasn't a whole lot he could do with a lady, if you see what I mean.'

'So your master was ill when he arrived in Chartres?'

'How did you know that? He got soaked when we were fording a river and had a fever by the time we got here. The innkeeper sent him to a woman physician who lives nearby. A fine young thing she was, too, but not one with any time for a bit of banter. She tended to the master and gave me a slap and said she didn't like my manners. And I'd only been trying to see if she really was as well-rounded as she looked. By the time we had carried Ogier back to the inn, it was nearly me that needed treatment! I tell you, the wind was so cold I had ice in my blood!'

'I thank you, sirs. Enjoy your wine,' said Galeran, who could well imagine Ausanne ridding herself of this unsavoury character.

25

Above the woollen hill stands the silk cathedral. Éloïse weaves fast, often working by candlelight to finish a motif before going to bed. Fatigue marks her young face. She has chosen a range of blue threads to match the colour of the sky with that of the stained glass. The tapestry portrays the cathedral as seen from above, by a bird perhaps, or by an angel. Éloïse spent many hours talking with the Bishop and with the master foreman before beginning her work on the future cathedral.

The windows of the narthex seem to have a life of their own. The sculpted columns she saw on the ground in the street are already in place on the Royal Portal in her work. Since she began the tapestry, Éloïse has ventured outside but once a day, and that is to gaze at the cathedral of Notre Dame. She stands before it, drawing furiously with a charcoal crayon on her oak board, and then runs home to transfer what she has seen onto the cloth.

26

The day was dying, the light fading. In the distance could be heard the rattles of men-at-arms gathering for their watch. The last workers were filing out of the cathedral. Notre Dame was soon isolated from the world of men and seemed to float through the moonlight like some great vessel.

Galeran returned to Audouard's house to find Hermine at work in the kitchen.

'My dear, have you seen your brother today?'

'No, I haven't,' she replied, a worried look on her face. 'He should have been home by now. It's almost dark.'

The knight was also worried, as well as exhausted from his busy day. But he did not show it. He smiled at Hermine.

'Come, come, my dear. There is nothing to be alarmed about. We shall wait for him together.'

He fetched his arms from the bedroom, sat down on a bench and hummed as he polished them. It was with some relief that he heard, a few moments later, Audouard's footsteps in the street.

The glazier brutally swung open the door and staggered in as though drunk. Galeran knew there had been some new drama. He jumped up to help his friend, guiding him to a bench. Audouard collapsed onto it, and sat with his head in his hands and his shoulders shaking.

Galeran exchanged a brief look with Hermine, then fetched a goatskin of strong liqueur he kept in his saddlebags.

'Here, drink this. It'll set you back on your feet.'

He threw a log on the hearth, and in silence all three sat and watched the wood catch fire and send a spray of sparks up the chimney. The colour came slowly back into Audouard's face, and Galeran felt he was now ready to answer some questions.

'So, what is it, my friend? Another misfortune?'

'My window . . . Somebody almost completely destroyed it last night. I've spent the day picking up pieces of glass. There are hundreds of them, smashed, strewn everywhere. And the leading has been torn out and twisted . . . '

For a moment Audouard looked like he could not breathe.

'Who would have done such a thing, and why?' Galeran asked softly.

'I have no idea!' cried the master glazier in despair. 'And I don't care! Yes! I do not care. You don't understand, I'll have to start all over again . . . I feel so old all of a sudden, so tired!'

He felt silent for a moment.

'This time it was no accident,' he went on in a low voice. 'It was a crime, a desecration. It was the forces of evil unleashed against Notre Dame!'

The knight looked down at the ground and said nothing. He knew there was more to this than gratuitous cruelty or commonplace malice. There was something stubborn and perverse here, something he knew well and whose presence he had felt since his arrival in Chartres.

Evil. Evil in its purest form, evil that sits at every feast and laughs at the misfortunes and sorrows of the world.

Galeran put his arm around his friend's shoulder.

'Come come, it is not like you to throw in the towel. As you said, we can see something positive in this incident since we now know that the war has been declared. For the first time the enemy has materialised. It is now up to us to find it.'

Audouard raised his head, and a vague smile came over his face.

'You are right. Forgive my weakness. But you know, that window . . . Such determination to destroy . . . '

'Listen, Audouard. I have an idea. Tomorrow, let me go up onto the scaffolding with your apprentices. I would also like to meet the stonecutter who lives on the site. You say he sleeps there, so he must have heard something. You cannot smash a window like that and make no noise. Have you spoken to him?'

'No. I couldn't find him.'

'So he has disappeared?'

'One of my men said he was seen leaving the cathedral, but that he came back again late in the afternoon.'

'Strange, for someone who is supposed never to leave the site. But listen, I have some mysteries to tell you, too.'

Galeran told of his visit to the Rovin Vignon, his interrogation of the jeweller's aides and his trip to the leprosarium. The only thing he did not mention was Ausanne's flight after he had made his declaration.

'Well, you certainly did not waste any time,' said Audouard. 'And you think all this is somehow linked?'

'I do not know. But one thing did strike me – the window in the jeweller's room.'

'Why?'

'It looks directly onto that part of the cathedral where all these incidents have taken place. It could, of course, be coincidence, but I think the old man may have seen something strange going on. Also, the jeweller had clients in both the Palais Comtal and Notre Dame. He sold garnets, sapphires and even opals. Who in the cathedral would have had the means to buy such stones?'

'I don't know,' replied Audouard. 'The Bishop, perhaps?'

'What about the chapter? Does it have much money?'

'They're tight when it comes to the building work. The master foreman has to account for his outgoings every single day. But as for the rest, I do not know. Perhaps all the money goes into the treasury of Notre Dame or Sainte-Châsse.'

Hermine had busied herself in the kitchen while the two men spoke. She had set the table, rekindled the fire in the little stone fireplace, and brought in a pewter jug of wine. A delicate aroma of herbs and of almond milk floated through the warm air.

'What delicious things have you made for us this evening, Hermine?' asked the master glazier, who was cheering up a little at the prospect of a good meal.

'Our Lady's Soup and herb pie. But come, Galeran, Audouard, we must begin. You know how quickly this soup goes cold.'

They sat down at the table. Hermine brought in the large, steaming pot of soup, a delicious white-coloured broth made of chicken, breadcrumbs and almonds. While the two men filled their bowls with the piping hot brew, Hermine slipped away back to her oven. She returned with the herb pie, over which she placed a cloth to keep it hot until the men had finished their broth.

'Please do not be offended that I am not eating with you. I dined earlier, and now I am tired and must sleep. There is some dried fruit in the pantry which you can have later.'

'Good night, sister.'

'Good night, sweet Hermine. It is a shame that you cannot share this sumptuous dinner with us. The soup is excellent, and my mouth is already watering at the sight of your pie. Now go and rest, and may Our Lady watch over your dreams.'

'Good night, Sir. Good night, brother.'

Hermine went towards her room, but then turned back with a conspiratorial air.

'You'll find the flask of hippocras in the small pantry.'

'Do not worry about us, my dear. Audouard and I shall not die of thirst or hunger this night. Sleep well.'

As though reluctantly, Hermine turned and went to her room, her apron a little lop-sided on her broad hips.

27

Ausanne, worn out after a day rich in diverse emotions, was hurrying to get back to her lodgings before the curfew was sounded. She had spent the afternoon in the Jewish quarter where the midwife had needed help with two difficult births. They had failed to save one of the babies. But both mothers were well, and Chartres could now count a pair of healthy twins among its inhabitants.

The torch Ausanne carried barely lit the ground in front of her. She went along Rue de la Boucherie, as she preferred to skirt the high walls of the Palais Comtal than to take Rue Evière. A student, who looked a little tipsy and whose torch swayed in his unsteady hand, approached her. She recognised him as the son of one of her patients, but merely nodded at him and rushed on, little inclined to conversation at this late hour.

She shivered, perhaps from fatigue, and pulled her cloak tighter around her shoulders. The streets seemed particularly steep this evening, and she stopped to catch her breath. The silhouette that had been following her also stopped.

The last shutters were being closed with a bang. Ausanne felt uneasy. She thought she had heard steps behind her but when she turned to look there was no one. Yet still she felt she was being watched.

'My God! Either I am going mad or I am exhausted. There is no one there.'

But she again heard footsteps as soon as she moved off. They were closer now and quicker, as though whoever they belonged to had resolved to catch up with her.

Ausanne, frightened now, decided it would be better to hide and prepare to face up to whoever was following her. As a child she had always been the slowest, and knew there was no point in trying to run. She went into a doorway and stood in front of her torch to try to mask its faint light. She took a stylet from her bag and held it ready. The footsteps drew closer.

A moment passed that seemed to her an eternity, and the

large figure of a man strode by, the light of his torch sweeping over the ground. He was so close that Ausanne bit her lips to stop herself screaming with fear. But he seemed in a hurry and was concerned only with lighting his path.

Ausanne heard his steps fade into the distance, and quietly emerged from her hiding place. The street was silent and deserted.

'What an idiot I am!' she thought. 'He wasn't following me.'

But, as a precaution, she slipped the stylet inside her cloak, gripping the handle tightly.

She was about to set off again when a strong hand grabbed her arm and dragged her towards a nearby lane. Her torch fell to the ground and the flame went out. Ausanne screamed and fought with all her strength to free herself. The man threw her against a wall. She responded by lashing out with the stylet that she had somehow managed to hang on to.

Her assailant gave a cry of rage as he tried to disarm her and stop her screaming. But Ausanne screamed all the louder and tried to stab the hands that were reaching for her throat. Her attacker, who had not expected such resistance, released her and withdrew with a growl.

Ausanne stood gasping for breath, her heart thumping, her eyes fixed on her adversary's dark silhouette.

'Help, by God! Help! Fire! Fire!' she managed to cry, remembering the people of Chartres' great fear.

'Bitch! I'll make you pay!' the man muttered.

His hands dripping blood, he ran off into the night. Ausanne collapsed against a wall, then gathered up what little strength she had left and began limping away.

Shutters were flung noisily open, and heads appeared to look out into the darkness. Inside the houses men hurriedly pulled on their clothes and hunted for their weapons. Bolts were drawn back on doors, people called out to each other as they ventured out in little groups, their torches held high.

But there was nothing to see.

'Where's the woman who called for help? Where's the fire? Did you see anything?'

'All I saw was someone running off in that direction. There is no fire. It's another stunt by those bloody students!'

28

The two friends were still sitting around the table when someone banged on the front door. A voice, which Galeran immediately recognised as Ausanne's, called out for help.

'Open up! Open up! Quickly, for pity's sake!' begged the distressed young woman.

Galeran rushed to the door. He found there an Ausanne so pale that he thought she was about to faint. Her smock was torn and her cloak was gaping open. He carried her to a chair by the fire and fetched her a cup of wine.

'Audouard, go and get a blanket, quickly,' he said. 'Here, Ausanne, drink this. Don't try to talk, plenty of time for that later. Breathe gently now. Yes, like that. You're going to be fine, I can't see any wounds.'

The knight gently wiped the sweat from her forehead while she drank. Audouard brought in a blanket and placed it around her shoulders. The wine soon brought a little colour back to her face.

'I thank you, dear knight. And you, Master Audouard,' she said, sitting up a little. 'Forgive me for intruding on you like this at night.'

'You are always welcome here, Dame Ausanne,' replied the glazier. 'But what happened? Do you know who it was that set about you?'

'I do not, Sir. I was attacked as I was walking along Rue de la Juiverie. I screamed and fought back and my attacker ran off. Then I, too, made off. But I was too frightened and too weak to go home alone. I hoped that yourself or the knight might accompany me.'

'I shall go with you, Madam, if it pleases you,' said Galeran. 'But rest here for a while. Could you see your assailant's face?'

'No. But he was tall and strong. And I am sure I wounded him with my stylet.'

'You are lucky to have escaped. Now, if you feel strong

enough, tell me exactly what happened, beginning with the moment we parted.'

Ausanne looked at him, a strange smile on her lips.

'From that precise moment?'

'I see you are feeling better. But please, tell me anything you think may be important.'

She began her account, but Audouard interrupted just as she was about to tell of the attack. The glazier had suddenly become pale again, and he spoke in a hoarse voice.

'Hellish! There is a curse on this town.'

Galeran knew how tired his friend was, and tried to quiet him. But Audouard grew more and more tense.

'Are the both of you blind? There's a madman about! Now he's no longer content with damaging the cathedral, but has begun attacking people, too. May God protect us!' he said, and left the room.

The door of the bedchamber banged, then silence fell on the house. Ausanne and Galeran, shocked at Audouard's vehemence, looked at each other. Galeran told Ausanne about the shattered window in the cathedral.

'I understand,' she said, nodding. 'Fear not, I shall not misjudge him. I know he is a reasonable man. It is difficult for someone like him, who seeks to bring clarity to the world, to understand the workings of darkness. I should not have spoken of my attack in front of him. But I did not know that his window had been broken.'

'Come and sit at the table, Madam. You must eat something to regain your strength. There is some of Hermine's delicious soup left. I shall heat it for you.'

Ausanne took a seat, and let Galeran serve her, little used as she was to being looked after with such solicitude. She ate all that the knight put before her.

'Drink some more wine, and then I shall walk you home.'

'Thank you, knight. I shall gladly accept your protection and your arm. Thanks to your care I am already feeling much improved.'

Galeran fetched his cloak and his sword. He helped Ausanne pull on her cloak, then placed his own around her shoulders.

'But I am not cold,' she protested.

'That is not the only reason why I wish you to wear it, Madam.'

And he covered her long, red plaits with his hood.

'There are not many women with hair as striking as yours. I do not want any further attacks on you this evening.'

He quietly closed the door behind him and took his companion by the arm, holding the torch in his free hand. They soon arrived at Ausanne's lodgings on Rue Percheronne. He released her arm and stepped back a little.

'Dame Ausanne, promise me you will bolt your door tonight.'

'Chevalier Galeran,' said Ausanne in a voice that trembled a little. 'Do not leave me yet. Please allow me to show you a little more hospitality than I did this morning.'

The knight hesitated.

'In any case, I think it will be some time before I am ready to sleep,' added the physician.

'Very well, but I shall leave as soon as you are feeling better.'

The young woman moved aside to let the knight enter the house. He used his own torch to light one that hung from her wall. Ausanne gently closed the door and pulled across a heavy curtain to keep out the cold evening air that crept in through the gaps in the wood. She watched pensively as Galeran set alight the twigs in the fireplace. Within a few minutes a blazing fire lit up the room. The delicate aroma of vervain and lemon balm wafted through the air. Ausanne invited Galeran to sit on a bench at the long table.

'I would like to make you my favourite drink, Sir.'

'Please, do not call me sir. Galeran will do, and allow me to call you Ausanne.'

'How can I refuse after the courtesy you have shown me, Galeran.'

She fetched a pot of honey and an earthenware jar filled with a mix of plants and seeds. With a mortar she carefully ground the mixture, added the honey and poured the lot into a copper bowl along with a little wine and some alcohol. She then heated the preparation over the fire.

The knight could not take his eyes off her. He stared at her delicate profile, her strong chin, the curve of her neck, the little locks of russet hair that caught the light, the clear skin. He clenched his fists, painfully aware that the woman was so close to him and that he did not know what he should do.

When her preparation was ready, Ausanne poured it into two stoneware cups and handed one to Galeran. The knight took it, and at the same time took Ausanne's hand in his own and thanked her in a rather hoarse voice. She quickly withdrew her hand as though she had placed it in a fire.

An awkward silence ensued, which Galeran broke by complimenting her on the strange drink she had made for him.

'I assume there is no point in asking you for the recipe? A secret, no doubt.'

'Yes, my secret.'

'And not the only one, Ausanne,' said the knight, putting down the cup with which he had barely wet his lips. 'I'd like you to tell me about a certain day in the year 1134. The fifth of September, to be exact.'

Ausanne turned pale.

'Why do you ask me that?' she asked in a pained voice. 'Why do you harry me? What have I done to deserve it?'

'Nothing, Ausanne. I swear I seek only to help you. But, like everyone else here, you are hiding something from me. I want to know what is going on in this town. In the past few days alone there have been both accidents and deaths, and I want to know why.'

'Since your arrival, in fact!' exclaimed the young woman.

'Ah, so that's it! You think I am mixed up in all this?' said the knight, his voice now hard.

Ausanne jumped up from her seat.

'Yes, that's it. I suspect you. I'm afraid you may be the cause of it all. You are a man of arms, and no one here, except Audouard, knows you. And you have this strange way of looking at people . . . '

'Calm down, my dear! I am neither coward nor murderer.'

He drew closer to her and spoke in a more gentle tone.

'I could be angry with you, yet I sense more anxiety than hatred in your words. Look at me, Ausanne, and tell me if I look like a murderer.'

The knight placed one hand on her shoulder and with the other lifted up her chin. He fixed his blue eyes on hers and waited.

'No, Galeran,' she replied, turning her face away. 'I do not think it is you, and I do not want it to be you.'

'It is not me. That I swear before God and before Our Lady. I am only trying to do good, Ausanne.'

At which the young woman began sobbing violently. The knight, troubled by her despair, took her in his arms and led her to a chair.

'Sit down and listen to me. You see, Ausanne, I think that what is going on is somehow connected to the Great Fire of 1134. What exactly happened in this terrible tragedy, when the gates of Hell suddenly seemed to have been flung wide open? You must help me discover the truth, for I think neither sorcery nor malediction was to blame.'

'Why me?' protested Ausanne.

The knight smiled.

'Because no one knows the town better than you. You walk its streets night and day to visit the sick. You visit every home, you watch over the dying and listen to their last breath. And also, my dear, because you were here on that terrible night, you witnessed events.'

'I don't understand, I don't know anything,' Ausanne murmured.

'Ah, but you do, my dear. Like a priest, you judge it wise to keep your secrets well hidden.'

'That is the duty of every physician,' she replied, sitting up straight.

'Without doubt. But people's lives are in danger.'

'But just what connection can there be? That awful night left only corpses and rubble, nothing more.'

'No, Ausanne, not only corpses. There were also many survivors!'

'What do you mean? Are you suggesting I was somehow mixed up in this crime? Oh, please! Do not make me think of that night! I don't want to, do you hear? I don't want to remember!'

'Very well, Ausanne,' said the knight, kneeling down in

front of her. 'You are exhausted. Let us speak no more of it. You are probably right, and I am mistaken.'

She calmed herself and wiped away her tears.

'Forgive me, Galeran. I don't know what I'm saying any more. Too much is happening too quickly.'

'It is I who should be asking for forgiveness. I did not seek to upset you.'

'I feel better now. But it might be best if you leave me. I must sleep.'

'One last question. Do you remember where exactly you were attacked?'

'I certainly do. I took shelter not far from where the Simon family lives, on Rue de la Boucherie. Why do you ask?'

'Oh, no reason. Are you sure you injured your attacker?'

'I even think I cut him several times. Mainly on the hands.'

'Good. Now I must leave, my dear. You need your rest. Forgive my brutality, and give a poor knight some hope that he might be permitted to see you again without being subjected to your wrath.'

'You will be very welcome here,' replied Ausanne with a smile. 'That I promise you. Be careful on your way home.'

'That I will,' said Galeran, taking her trembling hand and placing it on his heart.

He stood up and went to the door. Ausanne bit her lips and Galeran smiled hesitantly as he glanced back at her from the doorstep.

A branch snapped beneath his feet. Ausanne, who was about to hand him a torch, gave a little cry.

'Don't be afraid, it is only a little flower,' said the knight, bending down to pick up a branch of sweetbrier. Ausanne took the flower and hurriedly shut the door. Galeran heard her slide the bolt across.

On his way home he ran into a patrol of men-at-arms. The curfew was long past and the soldiers gripped their pikes when they saw the glint of Galeran's sword.

'Who goes there?'

'A friend,' replied Galeran calmly. 'I am a knight and my name is Galeran de Lesneven.'

'Throw down your weapons and come forward so we may see this friend!'

'No, dear sirs. I will come forward but, by my faith, I shall not lay down my sword!'

'Sergeant, sergeant, I recognise him! He's the one who found the drowned man's belongings. He's a friend of the Provost, let him go.'

'Very well,' replied the sergeant in a haughty tone. 'You may pass, knight. But don't let me catch you out again after the curfew or you'll rue the day.'

'Truly?' retorted Galeran, who had been about to go on his way but who now stopped. His voice had suddenly taken on an almost metallic tone. He stared the sergeant in the face. The soldier stared back for a moment, then lowered his head with a mutter. He gave a sign to his men and the patrol moved on towards the Prévôté.

The knight smiled and carried on his way. He soon reached the place on Rue de la Boucherie where Ausanne said she had been attacked. He held up his torch to see if he could find any signs of the struggle. A dark stain caught his eye at the entrance to a narrow lane. He lowered the torch, knelt down, and ran his hand over the ground.

'Blood, no doubt. So Ausanne did cut her assailant. But who could want to kill her? Was it a thief or an act of vengeance? The trail stops here. He's a cunning fellow, for he has wrapped something around his wounds so as not to leave any more traces. Or perhaps it was only a minor wound.'

Galeran, realising he would find no more clues, turned and went back to Audouard's house.

Ausanne cries out in her sleep. Her betrothed does not recognise her. She yells out his name, but he does not hear. He turns his vacant face to her, his burned hands covered in blood. She throws herself at his feet, but he pays no heed, and carries on walking towards the fire. Suddenly he grabs her arms and drags her along behind him. The heat is unbearable as they draw closer to the flames. Ausanne tries to break free, but he will not let go. His jaw set, he carries her into the fire. She feels her body burning as though in the fires of Hell . . .

Ausanne woke up screaming, her body covered in sweat, her hands seeking out the extinguished night-light.

PART FOUR

And the heaven departed as a scroll when
it rolled together.

Revelation 6, 12

29

It began with terrible cramps in her stomach. She staggered, doubled up with pain, and looked for a place to hide, like a wild animal that slips into a hole or under a bush when it knows it is about to die.

She swayed for a moment in front of a ruined house, her shoulders shaken by convulsions. The place was deserted save for a swarm of bluebottles. She went hesitantly in, moving from one room to another, dragging her feet through the wet grass. Wells of light broke through the thatched roof. Skirting round a pile of rubble, she lay herself down on the ground and let out a long groan. The wind whistled through the dark building.

The cramps grew ever more violent and ever more frequent. Her teeth began to chatter.

'I'm cold, so cold . . . How dark it is . . . ' She tried to stand up but the ground seemed to move beneath her. She retched and vomited in long, painful spasms.

She raised up her head to see a white light shining before her. Her limbs numbed by pain, she fell onto her stomach and began crawling jerkily across the room. A greenish foam had appeared at the corner of her mouth. The light was closer now, and blinding.

'Help! Help! I'm dying!' she cried. But she knew no sound had come from her lips. She stopped, face down in the grass, her face blackened by the earth, her hands clawing the ground. She retched again, and the vomit soiled her chin and hair. A final and terrifying convulsion seized her.

30

Galeran had slept badly. He dressed quickly and went to join Audouard for breakfast. The morning Angelus had not yet been rung. Audouard, his face grey and weary, seemed uneasy.

'Galeran, I am sorry about last night. I must ask both yourself and Dame Ausanne to pardon me. Did you offer her something to eat? And I assume you accompanied her home. I am not fit to welcome you here! I have offended you, and under my own roof!'

'You have nothing to repent, my friend. You offended neither of us. Ausanne asked me to tell you how upset she was to hear of what happened to your window. She grudges you not.'

Hermine busied herself with laying out victuals on the table while the men talked. Galeran looked at the spread and invited his friend to join him at the table. Hermine poured each of them a bowl of steaming goat's milk and cut thick chunks of bread which she placed in a wicker basket. But the hearty meal still could not shake the master glazier from his dour mood, and a curt nod was all the knight could get in response to his questions.

Galeran, a little irritated, placed a hand on his friend's shoulder and gently reproached him.

'Audouard, I am here to help you, not for any other reason. We established that last night, but you seem to have forgotten.'

'No, I have not,' replied Audouard peremptorily. 'But you see, some of my suspicions have been reinforced since my glass was destroyed. But I will not speak of them till I am certain I am not mistaken. It is too grave a thing. Also, I must admit that I lied to you yesterday.'

'What do you mean, you lied?'

'The day before yesterday, actually. I went out again after the curfew.'

'I heard you getting out of bed, like the other nights. But I didn't think you had left the house.'

'I went to the cathedral.'

The knight could not hide his displeasure as he waited, a frown on his face, for his friend's explanation. Audouard lowered his voice, as though to excuse himself.

'When I arrived at the palisade I heard a strange, dull noise. It sounded like a woodman's axe. I am not a brave man, God knows, but I began to run towards the cathedral. I was thinking only of my stained glass, you understand. I saw a dim light behind the windows.'

'Did you see anything else?' asked Galeran severely.

'No, but I knew somebody was attacking my window. But it was already too late, the damage had been done. When I arrived the ground was covered in broken glass and bits of leading. The light had disappeared when I looked up again at the scaffolding, and I never saw that devilish woodsman.'

'Why did you not tell me this yesterday?'

'I don't know. What with everything that's going on, I did not want to own that I had gone back to the cathedral after curfew. I pretended I saw the destruction at the same time as the others. When you arrived yesterday evening, I kept up the pretence.'

'Audouard, you must give up this dangerous game. I understand what led you to behave as you did, but I know there is some machination behind it all: the mason's death the day I arrived, the jeweller found drowned the next day, yesterday your glasswork destroyed, the attack on Ausanne – and God knows what will happen today! Do you want there to be other injuries and deaths?'

'By God, no, Galeran!'

'Then, by my faith, why are you not telling me all you know?' said Galeran, raising his voice.

Hermine, a little taken aback by the turn the conversation was taking, quietly left the room and went to seek some calm in the garden.

Audouard shook his head stubbornly.

'No, I want to be sure before I say anything. Please trust me. It is an affair between men of the same guild.'

The master glazier had regained his composure and now held the knight's unblinking attention.

'You mean you suspect a collegue of these deeds?' demanded Galeran.

'Do not put words into my mouth! Stay out of it for the moment, I beg you.'

The knight nodded.

'Very well,' he said dryly. 'But just for one day. I warn you that, whether you agree or not, tomorrow I shall have to step in.'

'Do not be offended, Galeran. I swear on my life that I shall tell you all this very evening, whatever it costs me.'

'Be careful, Audouard. And remember, blood always begets blood.'

'I must go. Adieu, Galeran.'

'Adieu, my friend. May God protect you. And do not forget that I shall come to the cathedral today as agreed.'

Audouard nodded and went to the garden to kiss Hermine goodbye. He gazed tenderly for a moment at his ageing sister. Despite the cool morning air, she had dozed off on the bench.

'Hermine, Hermine, I must talk to you.'

'Mmnn . . . Forgive me, brother. I wasn't sleeping, you know. I was just thinking,' she said. 'Tell me, are you really so angry with Chevalier Galeran?'

'No, Hermine, don't think that. Galeran is right, even if his manner is a little brutal. I am acting like a fool, but at the moment I have no choice. But you must promise to help me, sister.'

'Of course, Audouard. What must I do?'

'Take this and give it to Galeran if some misfortune should befall me.'

Audouard took a pouch from inside his glazier's smock and handed it to Hermine.

'Why are you so despondent, brother? Why do you speak of misfortune to your beloved old Hermine, who loves you dearly?'

'Farewell, sister. God shield you. And do not forget your promise.'

He embraced her, then turned and left the house. Hermine suddenly felt cold and pulled her shawl tighter around her shoulders. She held the leather pouch in her plump fingers and wondered if she should give it to Galeran right away. But no, she had made a promise. She stood up slowly, went to her room, opened the large trunk she had inherited from her mother, and hid the pouch between the flounces of a petticoat.

Galeran was still sitting at the table, staring into space, his face grave. He smiled when Hermine came into the room.

'Our talk scared you off,' he said. 'I got a little carried away, but I am only trying to help your brother. Wait here, I have something for you.'

He returned with the pretty tablecloth he had bought two days before, and handed it awkwardly to Hermine.

'Here. This is for you, my dear.'

'Oh, Sir! You shouldn't have . . . ' she began to stammer, her blue eyes bright with delight.

But Galeran, uncomfortable whenever emotion was being expressed, had already left the room.

31

The weather was sullen that morning, and a strong wind from the north swept through the town. It was not a day for strolling, and only those with business to attend to were to be found on the streets of Chartres. Galeran fastened his cloak as he hurried along.

He made a few detours through back lanes before arriving in Rue de la Bretonnerie, where he soon found the house where the Bretons of Chartres met. He gave a loud knock on the door and waited. A statue of the brotherhood's patron saint, Saint-Malo, sat enthroned in a stone recess above the door.

'What is it?' a toothless old woman asked him in dialect as she opened the door.

Galeran replied in the same Saint-Malo dialect.

'Galeran de Lesneven, Madam. I wish to speak with the master of the house.'

'Come in. I shall fetch him.'

A few moments later a man of about forty years, tall and broad in the shoulders, walked into the room. His deeply lined face, his dark eyes and his determined chin gave him a proud air. Galeran was surprised to see that he wore a monk's habit.

He looked the knight up and down very quickly, but Galeran felt this was long enough for the man to get the measure of him.

'Forgive me for disturbing you, and allow me to introduce myself,' the knight said. 'I am Galeran de Lesneven, son of Gilduin.'

'Robert le Breton. What can I do for you?'

The voice was deep and serious, the look direct.

'I have heard that your brotherhood commands great respect at Notre Dame. I need your help in an affair that threatens the work at the cathedral. But I see that you yourself are a man of the cloth, and doubtless you have heard of the recent events that have delayed work.'

'I have. I was told by Thierry de Chartres, for I am his

student at the college. My compatriots and I do, of course, take a great interest in the future of this town. For two reasons.'

A smiled flickered across his wrinkled face.

'Have you perhaps forgotten the legend, Chevalier Galeran? It recounts that the sons of Japheth, the third son of Noah, came and settled in Armorica, from whence the boldest ventured as far as Chartres. The second reason is that the sanctuary of Notre Dame has since the Norman invasions harboured the relics of Saint Tugdual, the Bishop of Tréguier. That should give you an idea as to just how closely our community follows what happens here. Now speak your mind. How can we help you?'

Galeran felt he could confide in this man who emanated strength and loyalty. Here was a man who knew how to lead other men.

'There are two problems to be resolved,' said the knight. 'Firstly there are the accidents at the cathedral and the mason's death, and secondly there is the murder of the jeweller they fished out of the Eure.'

'I heard about that poor man. I think I may even have met him once in Notre Dame. So you think it was no accident?'

'I am sure of it,' replied Galeran. He told the Breton of Ausanne's verdict.

'Indeed, it would seem to have been a murder. You might be interested to know that the man sold some precious stones to one of the goldsmiths in our brotherhood, a chap who does work for the cathedral.'

'I am a stranger here. Can you tell me where I may find this man?'

'Of course. His name is Mallon and he lives on Rue du Cygne. His talent has made him famous here in Chartres. Even in Paris they have heard tell of him, for he did some work for Abbé Suger. He's a little gruff, but I shouldn't think that will frighten you. As for the events at the cathedral, how can I help you there?'

'I want to know if something odd happened there about a year ago. For these incidents appear to have begun at that time.'

Robert le Breton's brow furrowed in thought.

'The workers,' he said.

'What do you mean?'

'At that time a lot of workers, and many master craftsmen too, came to our town from Saint-Denis.'

'Are you thinking of something in particular?'

'Yes. It was mainly master craftsmen, be they stonecutters or glaziers, who came to work on the Royal Portal.'

'Stonecutters?' Galeran repeated pensively.

'If you want to find out more you should talk to Téobald, a master carpenter who has been here for several years. He knows everybody. Tell him I sent you.'

'That I will do, Robert, and I thank you for your help.'

'You are always welcome here, Chevalier Galeran. Come back whenever you wish.'

They saluted each other. The knight asked the old servant woman for directions, and headed off towards Rue du Cygne to question the goldsmith.

32

A schoolboy, dressed in an austere grey smock, pointed out the goldsmith's when Galeran asked. It was situated on the ground floor of the house of the Boël family. A long table in front of the door was laden with bowls, plates, hanaps and ewers, all finely wrought. The grey light of early morning was reflected by the polished surfaces of pewter and copper.

'Good day,' said Galeran, greeting a young man who was tinning a piece of metal. 'I am looking for goldsmith Mallon.'

'What do you want him for?' replied the young man without looking up.

'To ask him a few questions.'

'He has no time for questions.'

'Let me be the judge of that. Tell him Robert le Breton commends me.'

'You should have said,' said the young man, and he stood up immediately. 'Follow me.'

'Well, well!' thought Galeran. 'That name certainly opens doors.'

He followed the young man into the goldsmith's atelier. The scratching noise of a chisel filled the air. Short and thickset, his hair grey and a vigorous air about him, Mallon was bent over a ewer of polished pewter, carving a woman's face into the metal.

'Master,' the apprentice said quietly.

'What?' thundered a stentorian voice, much at odds with the man's short build.

'This gentleman has been commended by Robert le Breton.'

'Well, then, pull up a stool. I'll carry on working as we speak. Why did Robert send you? Are you from our land?'

'I am not.'

'But you have an accent?'

'I am from Lesneven. But I have not come here to talk about the far end of the world. I need your help.'

'My help? How can a goldsmith help a knight like yourself,

if not to make him a scabbard for his sword? But I see you already have a fine scabbard. Your sword, on the other hand, looks a little light to me.'

'All the better for cutting with! But enough of that. I want to ask you about the jeweller who sold you some precious stones.'

'Which one?' interrupted the goldsmith. 'I deal with many.'

'This one had, apart from sapphires and garnets, some gems that came from Hungary.'

'Ah! That was Ogier, Ogier de Reims. Ah, yes! Only Ogier could have come up with such stones. Ice blue stones, he called them.'

'Did you buy some from him recently?'

'Yes, but not directly. He was sick and sent a girl with the gems.'

'A girl?'

'Yes, and I'm not one for looking at women, but I have to say she wasn't much of a specimen!'

'When did she come?'

'Monday, I think.'

'Are you sure? And it was the girl who told you the jeweller was sick? What did she look like?'

'No bosom and no bum, if you see what I mean. A stick of a girl! She kept her head down the whole time. I gave her the pouch for Ogier and she put it in her bag without even checking how much was in there and ran off. I did wonder why Ogier hadn't sent one of his men. But then, that wasn't any of my business.'

'Can you show me the stones she brought you?'

'Why not?' said the goldsmith, and he turned to a little cupboard which he opened with a heavy key that hung at his belt.

'Here,' he said, handing over a red leather pouch. 'I must remember to give the pouch back, it belongs to Ogier.'

'Don't bother. It won't be much use to him.'

'What do you mean?'

'You obviously don't pay much attention to what goes on in your town.'

'Huh! If I were to listen to all the gossip, I'd never get any work done,' muttered Mallon.

'Ogier was murdered, and probably before you bought these stones,' said the knight as he let a handful of opals slip through his fingers. '"There is in them fire more gentle than that of the carbuncle, or of the brilliant purple of the amethyst, or the deep green of the emerald . . . Some are like the painter's palette, others resemble the flames of burning sulphur . . . " Pliny the Elder was right, these stones are extraordinary. But I think murder is too high a price to pay for them.'

'Murdered! And you think the girl might have killed Ogier to steal his gems?'

'No, not her. But I think I know what role she played. Mallon, tell your apprentice to take over the shop and accompany me to see the Provost. He must be told of this.'

Mallon barked some orders, locked his atelier and followed Galeran, grumbling all the time. The day had started badly for him. The two men did not speak as they picked their way through the stalls on Rue de la Pelleterie.

33

The Prévôté, a long, low building, was one of the few edifices in the upper town made of stone. A narrow street separated it from the Palais Comtal. Its walls were dotted with loopholes, and the passage leading into the building through a large oak gate stank of urine and defecation. A man-at-arms in a coat of chain mail escorted the two men to the Provost's quarters. A booming voice responded to the soldier's knock on the studded door.

'I said I didn't want to be disturbed!'

The door was flung open violently and slammed against the wall.

'Ah! It's you, Lesneven. Come in. And you too, don't stand there in that stinking corridor!'

Galeran, unimpressed by the Provost's agitation, entered, followed by the reluctant goldsmith. The room was small and colder than the corridor. Some daylight filtered in through the bars of a loophole high up on the wall. A rickety fireplace spat its smoke into the room. A jug of wine, an overturned cup and a set of knucklebones lay on the floor. A camp bed, a table and some benches constituted the only furniture. A cap and some breeches were piled on a stool to dry in front of the hearth.

'Sit down. Do you want something to drink? I think there's a cup here somewhere.'

'No, thank you. Please listen to what Mallon has to say.'

The goldsmith repeated what he had told the knight just a few minutes before.

'What are you saying?' roared the Provost. 'A girl came and sold you the jeweller's diamonds?'

'That's right, Sir,' the goldsmith replied dryly, aggravated by the Provost's contemptuous tone and boorish manners.

'And you don't know who she was?'

'I told you I had never seen her before.'

'And what do you make of this, Chevalier Galeran?'

'I think we should confront the jeweller's assistants and the innkeepers with Master Mallon.'

'Mmnn . . . Wait here, both of you!'

The Provost marched out of the room, slamming the door behind him.

Galeran and Mallon sat and watched the fireplace sending its smoke back into the room. The midday Angelus rang and the Provost had still not returned. An hour went by, and not a word had passed between the knight and the goldsmith. Galeran paced up and down the room like a bear in a cage. Mallon grumbled to himself about soldiery in general and the Provost in particular. They were beginning to think the Provost had forgotten them when they heard loud footsteps outside the room. The door flew open to reveal the Provost accompanied by the jeweller's assistants. The Provost's face was a bright red, which did not augur well.

'Impossible to get anything from these dolts. La Doëtte has gone out. Jehan asked a neighbour to look after the inn for him and has gone out too. And for once he's taken his wife with him. They've gone to the horse market in Maintenon. I've sent two horsemen to get him. So what shall we do with you two fellows?' he said, turning to the terrified assistants.

'Sergeant, put them in the cellar for the moment. They know the way!'

The sergeant grabbed the protesting pair and manhandled them out of the room, cursing and kicking them as he went.

'Sir Provost,' said Galeran, 'I promised Master Audouard I would meet him at the cathedral. You can send someone to fetch me if you need me again.'

'Very well. You may leave also, Master Mallon. I'll send someone for you, too, when we lay hands on the innkeeper and his wife. On my honour, we shall soon get to the bottom of this.'

34

The workers had been battling since morning with the gusts of the north wind. It had eased for a while around midday, but now again unleashed its wrath upon them. The glaziers and the stonecutters on the Royal Portal bore the brunt of it, and struggled to get any work done.

The carpenters who had been putting chevrons in the tower had already given up, for it had become impossible to maintain a grip on the forest of wooden beams soaring up towards the sky.

Clouds of dust billowed around the ground. The wind flung canvas covers and planks up into the air and deposited them several yards away. Work on the cathedral was slowing down, and the sculptors on the Royal Portal were reluctant to carry on. The master foreman marched about, enjoining his men to take extra care. He was ready to halt work completely if the wind grew any stronger.

Galeran could hardly distinguish the outlines of the building through the swirls of dust. He walked past a group of carpenters, their ropes slung over their shoulders. Two of them were speaking in Breton, and he recalled Robert le Breton's advice that he should seek out the old master carpenter from Saint-Malo.

'Excuse me,' he said in the dialect of that region, 'I am looking for a man named Téobald, a master carpenter by trade.'

The two men, one young and blond and with eyes the colour of the sea, the other old and white-haired, looked Galeran up and down before answering.

'What do you want with him?'

'I want to speak to him. Robert le Breton commends me.'

'Ah! You should have said!' said the older man, a smile ruffling his wrinkled face. 'He's standing right in front of you, is Téobald.'

'I am Galeran de Lesneven. I would like you to tell me about the stonecutters and the glaziers who came here from Saint-Denis.'

'I'm not a great one for talking, you know, but I'll tell you what I can. The glaziers, apart from Audouard and Théon, I don't know too well. But stone, that's a different thing!'

The old Breton turned around and began walking, with Galeran in his wake, towards the Royal Portal. He stopped in front of the central opening and pointed to the statues carved into the columns.

'You can know a man,' he said quietly, 'by looking at what he makes with his hands. Come closer and see how beautiful it is. This stonecutter has managed to make the heart of these stones beat! Look at his Moses clutching the Tables of the Law! Look at this queen with her long plaits! She is more nymph than woman!'

The old Breton carried on talking as he ran his fingers lovingly over the sculptures. But Galeran was no longer listening, for his eyes were devouring the queen of stone.

'Touch the stones, Sir, and you shall have the answer to your questions. I see you too are in love; you shall have your beloved's answer if you touch them.'

'I thank you, Téobald, but I already have my answer, even if it is not the one I hoped for.'

They saluted each other, and the knight took his leave of the old carpenter. Narrowly avoiding two workers running to pick up a ladder blown over by the wind, Galeran headed for the master glazier's atelier.

The glaziers were also feeling frustrated for the bad weather made it impossible for them to put any of their stained glass in place. Audouard, his face tense, watched his assistants cut blue glass with a red-hot iron.

Galeran shook the dust off his clothes when he entered the atelier, then went to warm his hands over the brazier. Audouard nodded to him, and continued to watch his apprentices' delicate manoeuvrings.

'Watch what you're doing there! Are you asleep?' he cried, grabbing the iron out of one of the men's hands. 'Cut it here!'

Then he handed back the iron and turned to Galeran.

'Given how pigheaded you are, I suppose you still want to go up with us on the scaffolding? You have chosen your moment badly. This is not the weather for climbing.'

'Yes, I see that.'

'You haven't seen anything yet! At one hundred and fifty feet you're closer to Hell than to Heaven. Let us go, then.'

The two men braced themselves against the wind as they left the atelier, and had to shout to make themselves heard above the roar.

'It's getting worse!' cried Audouard. 'I left three of my men up there, I have to get them down!'

Galeran followed the glazier as he made for the tower.

'The carpenters have come down already, I saw them leaving the tower. We'll take the spiral staircase. From there we can walk along the scaffolding that leads to the stained-glass windows.'

'You usually make your men use the scaffolding to come down, don't you?'

'Yes. The staircase is for the masons and the carpenters working on the spire. But we can use it if there is strong wind or rain.'

The spiral staircase was vertiginous, its steps unguarded by any rail. It grew as the steeple grew, and would soon reach over three hundred feet.

Audouard climbed slowly, occasionally pressing himself against the wall to let a worker pass. Galeran followed close behind. The wind whistled through the gaping windows high in the cathedral.

'I don't know if we'll be able to stay up there long, this wind is too dangerous!' shouted Audouard. 'Follow me. We shall go over the gates of the Royal Portal.'

They left the staircase and walked across some planks that led to the scaffolding where the master glaziers worked.

'Be very careful. Watch out for sudden gusts and grab onto something if you feel unsteady. It's like being on a ship in a storm here. If the Angelus bell rings, then we must go down immediately. Those are Thiberge's orders. He prefers to lose a day's work than to lose a man.'

They passed by stained-glass windows depicting the Passion

and the Childhood of Christ. Galeran stopped to wonder at the striking mix of burning red and deep blue.

'Beautiful, is it not?' said Audouard. 'It was made by Théon, a glazier who also worked with me at Saint-Denis. He is making faster progress than me,' he added with a note of sadness in his voice.

When they arrived at the Jesse tree, Galeran admired the most supernatural blue of his friend's creation. Nearby stood a pile of broken glass and twisted metal that came from the part of the window that had been destroyed. A worker was sorting through the debris before storing it in a chestnut crate.

A piece of blue glass glowed as it lay on the wooden planks. Galeran picked it up and held it in front of his eye. As he surveyed Notre Dame through the glass splinter, he spotted a slim figure close by who seemed to be staring at him.

'It's a piece of glass from the Jesse tree,' said the apprentice who was picking up the pieces. 'Only Audouard knows how to make this pigment.'

'Really?' asked Galeran, lowering the glass from his eye and looking at the place where he had seen the figure.

But there was nothing there. It was as though the man existed only through the magic of the blue glass. Galeran put the shard in his pocket.

'There are bits everywhere,' continued the apprentice. 'Someone went to a lot of bother wrecking the window. But who? I just don't understand it. And the other glaziers say they saw nothing! A friend of mine, a labourer, has also had his work destroyed. We might have to put guards here at night. Maître Enguerrand sleeps here on the site, but he says he heard nothing the night it happened. I think he might have a mistress he goes to see at night.'

'I'll give you a hand,' said Galeran, stooping to gather up some pieces of glass. 'Tell me some more about this Enguerrand.'

'Well, he's a stonecutter. He's working on the statues on the portals and on a sculpture in the tower. The master foreman lets him live up here in a little cabin. When the weather allows it he even sleeps out in the open alongside the crows and the sparrowhawks. He has taken a vow of solitude.'

'Indeed?'

'That's what they say. I think he's a little mad, but I own there's not another sculptor to match.'

'That's what Master Audouard says. So he actually lives up here?'

'That's right. He has made himself a shelter on a gangway inside the tower. I often wonder how it manages to withstand the wind. In any case, that's where he is whenever he's not working in his atelier down below.'

'Where is it?'

'Climb up those girders in front of you there and you'll get to the steeple. Then take the staircase again. You'll have to do quite a bit of climbing. You'll see his hut just before the very top of the spire.'

Audouard, who had gone on ahead of the knight, returned at that moment and brusquely sent the apprentice off to join his colleagues.

'Didn't you hear me calling? Everyone has gone down, it's too dangerous up here. Take your crate and go!'

The young man's face turned red. He made his excuses and left.

'I've sent all my men down. With this weather I don't think it will be long before Thiberge decides to stop work. I'm going to have one last look around, then I have to go to Marchenoir forest with Thibaud. We have to get some glass from the ateliers there.'

'You have an atelier in Marchenoir?'

'Yes, that's where I make my glass. Théon and I built it. We have just one furnace but two ateliers there. And we have a house where we can spend the night if we need to. I have two men there all the time.'

'Let us go down, then,' said Galeran. 'I shall take the staircase, and we shall meet below. I might even decide to get my horse and accompany you to the forest!'

Galeran left his friend and set out for Enguerrand's hut. He passed a mason coming down the stairs with a hod on his shoulder. He climbed and climbed and climbed. The stairs seemed to go on for ever, but he eventually saw above him the dark form of a platform bearing what looked like a hunter's cabin. A series of long planks covered with tar were set against the wall.

'There's barely enough room for a man to stretch out in there,' thought the knight.

He was just about to climb onto the platform when a sinister cry echoed through the building. At that very instant the bells announcing the evacuation of the site began to ring. The violence of the storm had forced the master foreman to stop all work. The yells of the workers at the Royal Portal could still be heard despite the noise of the great bell.

Galeran bounded down the steps three at a time. A worker, standing at the start of the gangways that led to Théon and Audouard's windows, was shouting something that the knight could not understand. The scaffolding was deserted. All that could be seen was a piece of blue cloth in the passageway. His face furrowed against the wind and the dust, Galeran moved towards the cloth. He had recognised the sky-blue colour.

He stopped for a moment, horrified by what he saw, then stumbled forward again towards the body that lay at the bottom of the ladder.

The master glazier was slumped against a panel of glass. His long smock was blowing in the wind. Blood that seemed all too red spread over the shards of blue glass.

Galeran took hold of his friend's body and dragged it out of the wind. He carefully turned it over and removed the fingers that gripped a long blade of glass embedded in its chest. Blood suddenly spurted out, and, although Audouard's breath still came in rapid little gulps, Galeran knew that his friend was lost. The glazier was trying to say something through the bubbles that were forming at the corner of his mouth. A faint murmur finally emerged from his lips.

'Aus . . . tell Aus . . . '

His head slumped, his eyes still wide open and staring up at the sky. The glazier had surrendered his soul to Notre Dame.

Galeran stood and looked at his friend for some time. Then he heard footsteps. The workers had told the glazier's men and they had come running.

'Do not come any closer, and do not touch anything!' said Galeran without turning round. 'Fetch Dame Ausanne and the Provost.'

The men stopped short. The knight knelt down and gently closed his friend's eyes. An eerie silence now reigned on the site. Even the wind seemed to have abated. Groups of men formed without a word on the scaffolding, on the ladders, the platforms, in the staircase. Galeran stood up slowly, took off his cloak and placed it over Audouard's lifeless body.

35

The workers moved quickly aside to make way for the Provost and his men.

'Well, Chevalier Galeran,' said the old soldier, 'we meet yet again in less than pleasant circumstances. Is he . . . ?'

'Yes, Sir Provost,' said the knight. 'My friend is dead.'

The workers parted again, this time for Dame Ausanne.

'Galeran? Oh my God! It's Audouard!' she cried, for she had not been told who the dead man was.

'Everyone move aside!' she said severely.

The men-at-arms and the workers did as they were told, and Ausanne bent down to examine Audouard. Removing Galeran's cloak, she looked the body up and down with disconcerting calm. She took his hands and looked at his fingers. Then she bared his chest, took a pair of tweezers from her bag and removed the long piece of glass, placing it carefully on a piece of cloth she had laid out on the ground by her side.

'Where were you, Chevalier Galeran, when the accident took place?' she suddenly asked.

'In the tower. Why do you ask?'

'To see if you know how the accident happened.'

'But I do not see how you can "accidentally" get a piece of glass stuck in your heart!'

'We shall speak of that later. Now please let me carry on with my examination,' she said peremptorily. 'This death is too close to you for you to be a good judge, believe me!'

Galeran withdrew, his face sombre. He made his way through the crowd towards the staircase, but there he stopped short. The man he had seen through the blue glass splinter stood before him. He wore a long grey smock, scars ringed the eyes that lay sunk deep in their sockets, and his thin beard did little to hide the hideous marks on his cheeks. Galeran went towards him but before he could take a step the man had disappeared into the half-light of the stairwell. The knight ran after him, but could see no one when he reached the stairs.

'It looks like he has gone out onto the scaffolding despite the storm,' thought Galeran.

He went back to Ausanne and told her he would go and break the news to Hermine.

'Oh no, let me do that. It is better coming from a woman. You men are never good at such things. Besides, poor Hermine will most likely need my care.'

'You are right, Ausanne. I own I would be less talented for such an errand,' said Galeran, squeezing Ausanne's hand.

Ausanne had almost reached Hermine's house and still did not know how she would tell her of her brother's brutal death. She gave two soft knocks on the door, and was trying to choose her words when Hermine arrived.

'Something has happened to my brother,' said the old woman calmly when she saw the physician's pale face.

'Yes, Hermine,' replied Ausanne. 'He had a fall. I am sorry, but there was nothing we could do for him.'

Hermine swayed for an instant, then quickly regained her composure.

'My brother is dead. Take me to him.'

'Galeran sent me to you. He would like you to take this tonic. I promise you we shall bring your brother here so that you may pay your last respects to him.'

'Very well,' said the old woman, obediently taking the phial the physician handed her.

A large tear trickled down her cheek, marking the onset of a long and silent despair. Hermine was on her own now, and she knew it. The man who had shown her such tenderness and to whom she had given so much was gone, and gone for ever.

'Is there someone you'd like me to fetch?' asked Ausanne. 'A neighbour? Should I get Bertrade? You two are good friends. I don't want to leave you on your own.'

'I would prefer to be alone now. But please tell the knight to come and see me. I have a message for him.'

'A message?'

'This very morning Audouard, may the Lord and Our Lady have mercy on his soul, told me that misfortune might befall him. He wanted me to give a pouch to Galeran if it did.'

'Give it to me, Hermine, and I shall make sure the knight gets it. It may be important.'

'I don't know . . . My brother told me to give it only to the knight. But Audouard was very fond of you.'

'And I of him, Hermine. I loved the man.'

'But not as he loved you. Of that I am sure. For him, you were more than a woman! But I beg you, tell the knight to come here and not to fret over my sorrow. I want to give him the pouch in person. A promise made to a dead man is doubly sacred!'

'You are right, my dear,' replied Ausanne, troubled by the old woman's words. 'But do please go and rest a little.'

'I shall. Go back now and do not worry about me,' said Hermine as she removed herself to her beloved kitchen garden.

Ausanne closed the door behind her and trudged off, her brow furrowed.

36

Galeran was wandering aimlessly around the cathedral when he bumped into Sergeant Geoffroy.

'The Provost would like to see you, Sir. The innkeepers have been found, and we have sent for Mallon.'

'Very well. I shall follow you,' said the knight wearily.

A large crowd had gathered in front of the Prévôté, much of it made up of workers from the cathedral. The men-at-arms guarding the heavy door moved aside at a sign from Sergeant Geoffroy. A hubbub of voices and footsteps filled the building. The Provost had wasted no time in gathering to him the various representatives of authority.

In the vast assembly room were to be found the Lord of Marmoutiers, Vicomte Georges, who spoke on behalf of Thibaud IV, the Lord of Puiset, two vicars, and Robert le Breton, who represented Bishop Geoffroy de Lèves.

A little to one side the jeweller's assistants stood next to Ausanne and a miserable old woman whom Galeran did not recognise.

All proceeded to seat themselves as best they could, on the few benches and stools available, along the length of a trestle table.

Galeran nodded a greeting at the assembly and took a seat next to Robert le Breton, who told him who all the worthy people were.

'And who is that woman next to Ausanne?'

'That's the old woman who lives by the river. It was apparently Ausanne who had her sent for.'

The Provost banged the table with his fist.

'Silence!' he ordered. 'Bring forward the innkeepers.'

The heavy step of men-at-arms was heard and Mahaut was dragged before the judges. She fell onto a bench, her hair dishevelled and her dress torn, but her great beauty untarnished. Her heavy-lidded eyes flew around the room, from the great door to the high windows, as though desperately seeking a way out. Then she stood up to look at the assembled notables, examining in turn each of the severe faces turned towards her. When she saw the old woman sitting next to Ausanne, her eyes registered a brief moment of disgust and then turned away.

Then her husband, his face bloody, was hauled in and flung onto the bench next to Mahaut.

'These are the facts,' declared the Provost. 'Mallon the goldsmith and other witnesses tell us that Ogier de Reims has come to our town to sell his jewels each year for the last five years. He arrived last week for his annual visit and stayed in the Rovin Vignon, which has been owned for the past year by Jehan and Mahaut of Toulouse.'

Here he pointed at the unhappy couple.

'On Tuesday morning,' he continued, 'Ogier's body was found floating in the river.'

A murmur ran through the crowd.

'Dame Ausanne says the state of the body showed he had been in the water since Sunday at least and that he had been murdered. His head was smashed open.'

The murmur grew louder.

'Silence. I have not yet finished. Mallon further tells me that on Monday a woman came to his shop to tell him Ogier was unwell and that she was there to sell his stones for him. And when I wanted to question the innkeepers, who had not said anything about their guest's disappearance, they had fled.'

'That's not true!' protested Mahaut. 'We were going to the Maintenon market.'

'Truly? Then how is it that my cavalrymen caught up with you beyond Maintenon? And why is it that you had a considerable sum of money on your persons? And why did you resist when my men came to take you back?'

'We were afraid,' said Jehan. 'We didn't see your men's uniform under their cloaks. As for the money, it is mine. And we had only gone beyond Maintenon because I wanted to show Mahaut the gems without any prying eyes around.'

'You were right to be afraid!' retorted the Provost as he emptied a pouch onto the table in front of him. 'Where did you get all this money from? Prove to us that it didn't come from selling the gems.'

There came no reply. Galeran stood up to address the Provost.

'May I put some questions to the accused?'

'You may, knight.'

'Jehan, when did you see Ogier for the last time?'

'I've already said it was on Sunday.'

'But what time? Morning or evening?'

'He ate at the inn at midday and then went out. He came back before the Angelus for his dinner. Then he went to his room. We thought he had gone to bed, but he knocked on our door and said he had to go out again. It was my wife who let him out. And that was the last time we saw him.'

'So it was Sunday evening. La Doëtte told me the cloak he wore had been given to him by his late wife.'

Jehan made no response.

'It appears he was very attached to it,' said the knight.

'I see what the little pest is up to!' cried Mahaut. 'More of her lies. Ask the jeweller's men, they'll tell you Ogier sometimes went out without his cloak.'

'Mahaut is right,' said Robert, one of the two assistants. 'He often left it behind, in his room.'

'And on Sunday, when it was raining and he had just been ill, he went out without his cloak to go for a swim.'

'So?' snapped Mahaut. 'What he does is none of my business.'

She was on her feet now, snarling like a trapped animal. Jehan, for his part, seemed pensive.

'In any case,' continued Galeran, 'you were apparently the last person to see Ogier alive. Did you know, Dame Mahaut, where he hid his jewels?'

'Of course I knew!'

More than one person in the assembly gasped.

'Yes, I knew where the stones were kept! And they did, too!' she said, pointing at the two assistants. 'And so did La Doëtte.'

A heavy silence hung over the room. Galeran, perplexed, returned to his seat, and the Provost again took command of the affair.

'Jehan and Mahaut, do you wish to confess to the murder of this man?'

'We are innocent,' declared Mahaut. 'You can prove nothing.'

'What if the goldsmith were to identify you?'

'It was not me.'

'Mallon, do you recognise this woman?'

'No, it is not her,' replied the goldsmith. 'I would have remembered this one! The one who came was but a girl, and one you wouldn't look twice at.'

'Very well. So, Dame Mahaut, you sent someone to sell the stones and that's where all this money comes from?'

Mallon was eyeing the pouch lying open on the table.

'May I have a look, Sir?' he asked, picking up the coins. 'This money was minted in Paris.'

'So?'

'It is not mine. I paid the girl with coins minted here in Chartres by the Bishop, with the image of the Veil of the Blessed Virgin on them.'

'That is no proof, Mallon,' snapped the Provost. 'They had plenty of time to visit the money-changers! The rate is much the same, so they wouldn't have lost much and that way they would have covered their tracks.'

'I'm telling you it is my money!' Jehan suddenly cried, furious at these wranglings.

'Then tell us where it came from!'

'That is none of your business,' the innkeeper replied obstinately.

The Provost turned towards the lords and Robert le Breton.

'What do you make of this?'

After long consultations the Vicomte spoke out.

'We call for the judgement of God! Ordeal by fire.'

Robert le Breton stood up in his turn.

'We are against. He who kills a Christian spills the blood of Christ. We ask, in the name of the Bishop, for more time to investigate the affair.'

'Such a request is not within the Bishop's remit,' the Vicomte replied dryly. 'The corpse was not found within the grounds of the cathedral, and the case thus comes under the jurisdiction of Comte Thibaud. The affair will be decided by the secular powers. Moreover, a man of the church such as yourself cannot deny the value of God's own judgement.'

Robert le Breton sat down again, much displeased.

'Let us proceed with the ordeal. Have the irons heated,' the Provost ordered one of his men.

Mahaut began to shriek.

'Do not touch me! I am innocent!'

Then she turned and pointed at Ausanne.

'She is behind it all!'

Galeran jumped to his feet in anger.

'The wench is lying!' he cried. 'She would say anything to save her skin.'

The Vicomte approached Mahaut.

'You dare accuse Dame Ausanne?'

'You dared accuse me! I am certain it is her! She arranged everything with La Doëtte. The pair of them are thick as thieves! And she knew the jeweller better than me.'

Silence fell on the room again.

'She's lying,' said Ausanne, white with anger. 'What more can you expect from a woman whose own mother turned her out? Go on,' she said, addressing the old woman from the river, 'tell them she's your daughter!'

The woman got slowly and with some difficulty to her feet. Her face was hard and her voice shrill.

'Yes,' she said with a nod. 'She's my daughter, the strumpet. And she's worked in every whorehouse from here to the Orient!'

'So you also hate me enough to want me dead?' cried Mahaut. 'But I won't give you that pleasure: And why wouldn't I have told you, Sir Provost, about Ogier's disapperance? Have I not always told you when I had problems with my customers? How do you know it wasn't her that had the gems sold? And that La Doëtte wasn't her accomplice?'

Ausanne was livid and could find nothing to counter Mahaut's persuasions. Galeran watched the reaction of the assembly and felt that the innkeeper's wife was beginning to turn the situation to her favour.

'Sir Provost, allow me to put some more questions to the accused,' asked the knight.

'Please do.'

Galeran turned to the physician.

'Dame Ausanne, where were you on Monday?'

'I was at the leprosarium until late in the afternoon.'

'That is what Frère Gacé told me when I went to see him there. Ausanne is a good woman, and all of you here know that. She spends her time among the lepers, the ill and the dead. Do you really think she murdered an old man, a man whom she had nursed back to health? And just why would she have killed him?'

An approving murmur ran through the assembly. Galeran sensed the balance of opinion was swinging back. He turned to Mahaut.

'I saw you for the first time on Monday and you were wearing a veil. Were you returning from the money-changers, Madam? Do not lie, for it will be easy to find out. As Mallon said, men do not easily forget a woman like yourself. Even in a veil, or in sackcloth for that matter, your shapeliness betrays you.'

Then he addressed Jehan.

'Have you nothing to say?'

'No.'

'The Provost's men treated you gently, I see,' said the knight, looking at the bruises on the man's face. 'But I cannot see why they should have done that to your hands.'

Jehan cast him a furious look and hid his bandaged hands in his sleeves.

'Ausanne, please tell us what happened to you on Wednesday night.'

Ausanne told her story, and a buzz of whispers flew around the room.

'Do you think Ausanne can be both guilty and a victim?'

'My husband was taken by a fit of madness,' pleaded Mahaut. 'A couple of months ago I gave La Doëtte a beating that might have been a little too severe. She was always breaking things that I liked and play-acting around my Jehan!

That bitch Ausanne was always meddling in our affairs, and now she says we can't even punish our servants any more! So when Jehan saw her at the inn the other day with the knight, he'd had enough. But he only wanted to give her a fright. He slapped her, that's true, but then she starts lashing out with a knife!'

From beyond the thick walls of the assembly room came the clamour of the angry crowd that had gathered outside.

'Silence, all of you!' thundered the Provost.

And everyone was silent. Footsteps approached in the corridor. Galeran, like the Vicomte and the Provost, prepared to draw his sword. There was a violent knocking at the door.

'Open it!' shouted the Provost.

A man-at-arms opened the door and two young men bearing a litter marched in. On the stretcher lay a human form covered in a soiled sheet. The guard carefully closed the door behind them.

'Put it down over there,' said the Provost. 'And remove that sheet. Sergeant Geoffroy, go and quiet that mob out there! Take some men and break it up. Use your batons if you have to.'

One of the stretcher bearers removed the sheet and the assembly gathered round to gape. Its long hair muddy and its face filthy and twisted in pain, the body lying there was barely recognisable as that of La Doëtte.

'Where did you find her?' asked the Provost.

'We were out hunting rabbits, and we chased one into a ruined cottage, and that's where we saw her.'

'Very well. Leave us now, and wait outside.'

Galeran asked the Provost if he might have a private conversation with Ausanne, a request which was denied. The two men talked more, then the Provost called the physician to him.

'Tell me, Dame Ausanne, in your opinion, what did this girl die of?'

Ausanne knelt down beside La Doëtte.

'First impressions would suggest the falling sickness. She has had muscle spasms, her lips are white and she has foamed at the mouth. And she has vomited a lot. It looks as though her heart gave in. She was not of a strong constitution.'

Now Galeran knelt beside La Doëtte and examined her face as Ausanne gently closed the girl's eyes.

'May she rest in peace,' she said.

The knight suddenly stiffened and withdrew to his place next to Robert le Breton.

'Your neighbourts say Doëtte wasn't at her work yesterday evening,' said the Provost, turning to the innkeeper's wife. 'There seem to be quite a few people who die as soon as they leave your company, Dame Mahaut.'

'I tell you she was very much alive when I spoke with her yesterday! I even gave her what was left of the meat for her mother. But why don't you ask that one about it all?' she said, an accusing finger pointing at Ausanne. 'That great scholar knows more than all of us!'

The lords and the vicars deliberated at the other end of the hall.

'By our faith,' declared the Vicomte, 'we again call for God's judgement and ask that His light resolve this question.'

'So that I may be cleansed of any suspicion I demand that I be judged at the same time,' said Ausanne abruptly, her eyes fixed on the Vicomte.

'You are in no way obliged to do so, Madam,' replied the Vicomte. 'We do not believe you are guilty.'

'I insist. My family's name must not be sullied.'

Galerran clenched his jaw. He had seen many an ordeal and knew its agony and invariably deadly outcome. He stood up and went to Mahaut.

'Why have you accused her? Ausanne never did anything against you. If anything happens to her because of you I shall kill you with my own hands.'

'Listen to me, gentle knight,' said Mahaut softly, 'I have suffered too much in my dog's life to pay for a crime that I did not commit. I did not kill the man, do you hear? I swear it. I am a whore, as my dear mother has told you. Or at least was one until Jehan married me. Is it a crime to have been a harlot? Christ loved us, did he not? And who has not sinned?

But I have never killed and nor has Jehan! He is a good man, and the only one who has ever loved me. Believe me, knight, your judgement is clouded by your interest in this woman.'

'That's enough, Mahaut, we might end up believing you,' said Galeran as he withdrew.

Jehan sat on his bench, a defeated air about him, seemingly indifferent to what was being said. Two men brought in a crucible filled with glowing embers and placed it at the far end of the hall. Sergeant Geoffroy told the accused to prepare themselves.

'May God protect His own!' he said.

Mahaut began screaming as a soldier grabbed hold of her. Her old mother got to her feet and tried to go to her. But Mallon held her back, and she sat down again, her face buried in her hands.

Suddenly Jehan, as though wakened from a dream, jumped up and hurled the soldier against the wall. He placed himself in front of Mahaut, his face ugly with fury, his eyes blazing.

'I will kill anyone who touches her!'

The Provost called off the men-at-arms who were about to pounce on him.

'Leave him. Do you want to undergo the ordeal first, Jehan?'

'Yes,' said the innkeeper, himself seizing the red-hot iron in his bandaged hands.

A crackling was heard as the dressing began to burn. Soon the stench of charred flesh filled the air. But Jehan made no sound. He turned towards Mahaut, and his gaze held her magnificent green eyes. His hand was now fused with the scorching metal. He trembled, and sweat ran down his face. A voiceless groan came from lips he was biting so hard that they bled.

He took a step towards Mahaut, then fell to the ground, his eyes bulging. Ausanne ran to him and with a piece of cloth she tried to wrest the iron from his hand. But the burned flesh and the metal had become one. Mahaut brutally pushed her aside and flung herself on her husband's body.

'Sir Provost, this man is dead,' said Ausanne. 'His heart has given in.'

'You're lying!' shrieked Mahaut. 'Jehan, come back, I beg you! Don't leave me, Jehan!'

Her arms gripped the inert body, and guards had to pull her away.

Their hearts stirred by such horror, the members of the assembly stood dumbly as they watched this tragic couple they had just destroyed.

But life likes to make a mockery of human suffering, and at that very moment the door to the hall was flung open and a very young man appeared, with a dumbfounded look and big round eyes that rolled comically.

'And who is this?' demanded the Provost of the soldier who accompanied the youth.

'He says he's Doëtte's betrothed.'

'That's a new one! No one told me the girl had a betrothed. What's your name?'

'Gautier. I live with my family on the Saint-Chéron road. We're woodcutters. I was meant to meet my Doëtte but she didn't come. So I went looking for her. A boy from the upper town told me they'd found a dead girl. I wanted to see if . . . '

The Provost moved aside to let the boy look at the body on the litter.

'Doëtte! My Doëtte!'

He fell to his knees.

'What have they done to you? Why is she all twisted like that?'

'She had an attack. Now stand up and act like a man,' growled the Provost, rolling his eyes to heaven.

Gautier only now seemed to realise what place he was in. He looked at Jehan's body and at the irons and at the assembled worthies, and started to tremble.

'Have no fear. The irons are not for you. But tell me more about Doëtte and yourself.'

'I'll tell you everything. It happened on Sunday night . . . ' muttered the shivering boy.

'What happened?'

'I was meant to marry Doëtte. But we just wanted to touch a bit first to see if our bodies would take to each other. On

Sunday, after she went to see her mother, Doëtte didn't go back to the inn as she usually did. She came to meet me down by the Eure.'

'But it was raining that night.'

'Yes, but not all the time, and it wasn't cold. And Doëtte's body was nice and warm, and I had my cloak. We held each other very close . . . We spent the evening in the old wash house opposite the church of Saint-Hilaire.'

'And then?' demanded the Provost.

'Well, we saw them throw the body into the river. Right opposite us. There wasn't much light, but Doëtte could see that it was the jeweller. Even if he had no clothes on.'

'And did you recognise anyone else? Master Jehan, for example?'

The boy took a long look at the innkeeper's body.

'I know this man. I used to sell him firewood. But it's not the man I saw by the river. He was thinner. Doëtte said the woman was Mahaut, but I'd never seen her. When she pulled down her hood I could see she had two long plaits, like the ones those two women have,' he said, pointing at Mahaut and Ausanne.

'Doëtte knew what she wanted,' continued Gautier, 'and she loved me dearly! She wanted us to get married quickly, she wanted us to have children. And she told me she would have enough money for us to be happy for the rest of our lives. She showed me the money on Tuesday, when we met in the woods!'

'What?'

'She showed me the money. She had an awful lot of it in her purse. I've never seen so much!'

'Where did she keep her purse?'

'In her belt. She said no one would ever think she was carrying so much about with her. She was a crafty one, my Doëtte,' said the boy, who was now seized by long, painful sobs.

A man-at-arms guided him to a seat. The Provost leaned over La Doëtte's little body and moved aside the folds of the dress that covered the purse on her belt. He slid it off, placed it on the table, and opened it to reveal a pile of coins minted in Chartres.

A stupefied silence had come over the room. Robert le Breton was the first to break it. He approached the Provost, determined to bring an end to the macabre scene.

'Sir, what charge do you now bring against the innkeepers? A witness has told us it was not Jehan who threw the body into the river, that Mahaut didn't look much like Mahaut, and that the jewels were stolen and sold by this poor girl here, God rest her soul. The innkeepers' money does indeed appear to belong to the innkeepers, wherever they might have got it from. Now we must ask again who killed Ogier. And who would have killed him without wanting to rob him?'

He now turned to Galeran.

'Sir, I think we need your assistance.'

Robert le Breton crossed the room and stared the knight in the face.

'You and I both know which person in this hall did the deed.'

Galeran turned pale, then turned to face Ausanne.

'Madam, the dead have betrayed you.'

'What do you mean, Sir?' she exclaimed.

'I mean that you have committed certain errors.'

'No, Galeran! That accursed woman has betwitched you!'

'Alas, Madam, I wish that were the case, for it would mean you were innocent.'

Ausanne haughtily looked the knight up and down.

'I had nothing to do with all this,' she said.

'You are right. At least, not until this morning.'

Ausanne looked as if the ground had been pulled from under her feet. The knight fixed his clear gaze on her and spoke in a soft voice.

'Tell us who killed Ogier and I shall try to save you.'

His demand was met with silence. He turned to the Provost and repeated his earlier request.

'Sir, may I speak privately with this woman?'

'You may, Chevalier Galeran. I have sent for Frère Gacé to care for Dame Mahaut and to have these bodies given a decent burial. I shall have some wine brought in. I think we all need it. You may speak with Dame Ausanne in my room.'

Galeran took Ausanne's arm, forced her to stand up, and led her into the Provost's quarters. She fell onto the cot and stared up at the knight, as though transfixed.

'I am sorry for you, Ausanne. But, by God, why did you not confide in me the other night when there was still time? I could have saved you! It didn't take me long to realise that Mahaut and her husband, God rest his soul, were innocent. And you were, too, in your own way. But that was before I saw that poor child's body!'

'No, Galeran!'

'You poisoned her, didn't you? And I know the poison you used was mandrake, for I have seen it at its deadly work before.'

Ausanne sank her head in her hands.

'There were, of course, some signs suggesting the falling sickness, but it was clearly a case of poison. How could you do such a thing, Ausanne? And to a poor little girl who loved you?'

The knight received no reply.

'I realised what you'd done when you tried to close her eyes before I could get a look at them,' he went on. 'Only mandrake can turn the eyes such a fine yellow. How the child must have suffered, Ausanne! You lost your soul when you killed her, but I think that is what you wanted, is it not? Or perhaps you thought you could take a life and pay no price for your action?'

Ausanne sat motionless, staring straight ahead.

'I have taken you aside,' said the knight, 'not to talk to you about what we already know, but to discuss what the others should be told.'

'I understand,' said Ausanne suddenly. 'Accuse no one else but me, do you hear me? I alone killed!'

'You are lying, Ausanne! Do you not recall that you yourself told me after you'd examined Ogier's body that he had been struck by someone strong? And you couldn't even manage to turn his body over on your own! And what about the man that Gautier saw at your side? I suppose he was a phantom?'

'It was Jehan!' cried the physician.

'Don't try to tell me that, Ausanne. Jehan had eyes for one woman only, and that was not you. Leave him in peace. And what about the mason who fell to his death from the scaffolding? And poor Audouard, who died saying your name? Do you want me to believe that it was you who killed them?'

Ausanne cast her eyes to the ground.

'I am ready to face my death, Galeran,' she said. 'In that at least I shall not disappoint you.'

The knight gave her a curious look, and suddenly remembered his first visit to her house. He recalled the manuscripts carefully stored on the shelves and the luxurious credence table. But the thing that now came most clearly to his mind was the wooden bowl carved with the strange creature that was half-woman, half-demon. She had held it out to him as though it were some puzzle to be solved. Now, with Ausanne standing in front of him, he knew that she herself was the solution to the enigma.

He could now glimpse the infernal pride and force of will that had enabled this woman to escape the modest life of a weaver, teach herself the art of medicine and devote herself to the care of others. In just a few years Ausanne had carved out an empire for herself. She had reigned over the private life of a town, over the fears of hundreds of sick or dying townsfolk, over the secrets of tormented bodies.

How did she come to think that knowing how to give life also gave her the right to bring death? She has surrendered herself to the Evil One, thought Galeran with a shudder. She sold her soul! Ausanne was lost to him and to God. From now on when he looked at her red hair he would see only rust.

Galeran wiped the sweat from his brow and spoke in as calm a voice as he could.

'May Our Lady find clemency for you, Ausanne. Come and confess whatever you wish to confess, and I shall not contradict you.'

'Thank you, Galeran. If only we . . . '

'Stop, please!' groaned the knight.

Ausanne shook off Galeran's arm as she entered the assembly hall, and lifted her proud chin to face her judges.

'I alone am to blame. I killed Ogier and La Doëtte. Jehan was my lover, but he was innocent of any villainy, for all he did was help me dispose of the corpse. May he rest in peace. And may God forgive me, even if you cannot. May my punishment cleanse me of my sins.'

No one in the room had expected such a denouement. The Provost breathed heavily, and dared not look at Ausanne as he spoke.

'Take this woman and lock her in my quarters for the night,' he told his men.

Robert le Breton approached Ausanne.

'May I be of any assistance to you, Madam? Repent so that God may help you, for these men will not be clement. Do you wish my servant woman to stay with you this night?'

'There is no need, Sir. I prefer to be alone.'

37

Frère Gacé, who had come by horse with another monk from the sanatorium, was tending to the still unconscious Mahaut in a corner of the room. The old woman from the river was sponging her feverish forehead. Two men-at-arms had already carried out Jehan's body.

'This man had pride and courage,' said Robert le Breton, crossing himself. 'He died without a word. These ordeals are terrible things! How many innocent people have died for the sake of a few guilty men? If only they had been a little more patient. Time would have done what their violence could not.'

Galeran nodded in agreement. The men-at-arms had taken Ausanne to her improvised cell. She had walked out of the room as though she were a queen. The knight turned to the Provost.

'Well! We have heard how Ogier and Doëtte met their deaths, but the murders in the cathedral are still an enigma.'

'Of these I know not what to think.'

The remaining mysteries notwithstanding, the notables deliberated and delivered their verdict on Ausanne that same evening. A current of anger flowed through the town, with the workers threatening to abandon their labour at Notre Dame. The violent deaths had scared them, they saw the hand of the Devil therein. Men-at-arms marched through the town to pronounce the sentence on Ausanne:

Oyez! Oyez! Oyez! Gentle ladies and sirs,
The judgement of Bishop Thierry,
Represented by Robert le Breton, may Our Lady watch over them both!
By the grace of Comte Thibaud IV,
Represented by Vicomte Georges,
May Our Lady shield them!
By the grace of the Lords of Marmoutiers and of Puiset,

May Our Lady protect them!
By the grace of our good Provost,
May Our Lady watch over him!
Oyez! Hear the judgement pronounced on Dame Ausanne,
A physician residing in Rue Percheronne in our good town of Chartres.
For the murder of Ogier de Reims, a jeweller by trade,
And of La Doëtte, a serving girl in the inn known as the Rovin Vignon,
Dame Ausanne, by the grace of Comte Thibaud, may Our Lady protect him,
Shall be hanged by the neck until she is dead.
As is the custom, the Bishop requests that after the sentence is effected,
The woman's house shall be burned and its ashes dispersed
So that nothing may remain of the evil born in that place!
Oyez! Oyez! The execution shall take place before the assembled people
Tomorrow after the midday Angelus.

Galeran left the Prévôté accompanied by Robert. The cleric was silent, and Galeran dared not disturb his thoughts. He took his leave at the gate and strode off.

'Chevalier Galeran!'

'Yes,' said Galeran, turning around.

'Thank you for what you did. I know what it must have cost you. But tell me, why did Ausanne say Jehan was her accomplice? Who is she protecting? You know, don't you? There is too much passion in that woman, even if she has done much good. I think you would prefer to kill her with your own hands than see her hang.'

'Yes,' replied Galeran, with a lump in his throat. 'Even if she does deserve to die, I would not wish her to be hanged!'

He seized Robert le Breton's hand, held it for a moment against his chest, and then turned to walk away.

PART FIVE

Car nulle joie tant ne m'attrait
Que jouissance d'amour lointain
(For no other joy pleases me as much
As enjoyment of love from afar)

Jaufré Rudel

38

A dozen carts had arrived the previous evening and now formed a circle within the grounds of the cloister. They had transported the inhabitants of several villages that lay near the town of Blois. The pilgrims had left their homes some two months ago, and slowly made their way to Chartres with their offerings of wine and wood for Our Lady. Wisps of smoke rose up from the little encampment where they lay asleep, wrapped in their cloaks, on beds of straw. The women, the children and the infirm slept together in three of the carts, sheltered from the elements by sheets of canvas. The oxen that had pulled the carts nonchalantly chewed hay as they moved silently around their improvised enclosure.

An old man, his back against a barrel, his thin legs wrapped in bandages, sat and considered the cathedral. Often had he dreamed of this building, and now here it was in front of him, more magnificent than he could ever have imagined.

A canvas cover was drawn back and a girl of about ten years, her clothes in her hand, jumped down from one of the carts. Shivering, she quickly pulled on a pair of breeches, a long shirt, a cotton tunic and finally her wooden clogs. She gave a long sigh of relief, then, with a look of mischief in her eyes, shook herself as a young animal does as she turned to the old man.

'Good morning, Grandfather. I thought I was the first to rise today.'

'Oh no, my girl! But if you pass me my walking stick we can be the first at the cathedral for Prime.'

'Oh, please, Grandfather! And when shall we see her?'

'Who, Aubriette?' asked the old man, with a curious look at the girl.

She was small for her age, with a snub nose, brown curly hair and hazel eyes.

'*Her*! Notre Dame, of course!'

'Our Lady is everywhere in this town. Her house is here. If

you promise to be good, we shall go and see the Veil of the Blessed Virgin.'

'Tell me the story of the Veil again, Grandfather.'

'Sit down here next to me. You're making me dizzy!'

The girl sat cross-legged opposite her grandfather.

'The Virgin Mary is God's mother, and her Veil is kept here in Chartres. And this Veil is the one she wore when the Angel Gabriel came to her to announce the birth of Christ.'

'Oh!' exclaimed the child.

'The Veil is kept in a reliquary made of cedar wood that is plated with gold, studded with diamonds. It is protected by a golden griffon that was brought back from the Orient by the crusaders. And the reliquary is never, never, do you hear, opened!'

The girl looked at him wide-eyed, still filled with wonder at this story that she had heard so many times.

'And the Puits des Saints-Forts?'

'Ah, the well at Saints-Forts. They say that in the first century of our era the bodies of the first Christian martyrs were thrown into that well. Since then the water is reputed to have miraculous qualities. It is there that we shall bring our sick, and there that I myself shall lie down and ask to be healed.'

'You said you must spend a few days under the ground?'

'Yes, the women of the Saint-Lieux-Forts will care for us for nine days while the water performs its miracles.'

'Can I come and see you?'

'No. But you can say novenas to the Black Virgin.'

The girl considered a moment, then stamped the ground with her clogs.

'I shall pray to her every day that she may heal you!'

The old man, moved by these words, turned aside so that the girl should not see his emotion.

'Give me my stick. The Angelus bell is ringing for Prime. Look, the others are awake.'

39

At that same moment, in the vast crypt of Notre-Dame-Sous-Terre, a young woman begged for the salvation of a soul destined for Hell. She had been at the foot of the Black Virgin for several hours now. At first she had knelt, but felt this was not enough to gain the attention of the strange and severe little statue that had grown black with time. So she lay down on her stomach and flung her arms out in the shape of a cross, as she had seen many a penitent do. The cold of the flagstones slowly seeped into her body, numbing it, turning her lips blue, and throwing her into a state of semi-consciousness.

'Wake up, my child! Wake up!' cried the monk as he shook her.

The woman did not react. The monk shook her harder. Still she did not move. He took her arms and lifted her up with ease, for she weighed so little, put her over his broad shoulders and marched out of the chapel.

Some light trickled in through the tiny windows of the crypt. A long, vaulted corridor led directly to the Saints-Lieux-Forts. The subterranean hospital lay next to the well of the martyrs. The place was strangely silent. A score of beds lined the wall, with a drape hanging down between each of them. The vast room was lit by some torches and small oil lamps nestling in the walls.

A man, shaken by a cough, turned in his bed. A nurse helped him drink a little of the miraculous water. Nearby, another nurse applied fresh bandages to an invalid.

The monk recognised the second nurse and carried his charge towards her.

'Brother, what has happened? Who is this poor girl?'

'I don't know. I found her at the foot of the Black Virgin. Where shall I put her?'

'Follow me. There is a free bed over here.'

The monk put the girl gently down on the bed.

'Do you want me to stay?'

'No thank you, brother,' said the old woman.

She had already placed a blanket over the inert body and put some bricks to heat in a nearby brazier. The girl's eyes opened and she seemed to have regained consciousness. But she appeared indifferent to what went on around her. The nurse decided the most important thing was to warm her up. From under her tunic she took out a small phial and a wooden spatula and poured a few drops between the patient's gritted teeth. The girl began to cough, turned bright red and tried to sit up.

'You'll be fine, you'll be fine. Gently does it. Look, the colour's coming back to your cheeks already!'

'It's so strong!'

'A drop of eau de vie never did anyone any harm,' smiled the nurse as she took a brick from the brazier and wrapped it in a cloth.

'Here, girl. Put that on your stomach. That'll warm you up.'

The girl, touched by the old woman's kindness, suddenly burst into tears.

'It's all right, there's nothing to cry about,' said the nurse, stroking her hair.

'Oh, it's my poor sister. If only you knew.'

'Your sister?'

'Oh, nothing,' said Éloïse. 'I feel much better. I must go now.'

Then she took the nurse's hands and kissed them.

'I shall not forget your kindness. I shall pray to Our Lady for you.'

She threw back the blanket, slipped on her chausses and got shakily to her feet.

'You can't leave like that!'

The old woman, used to being obeyed, made her sit back down on the bed. She took from her bag a piece of bread and some dried meat.

'Here, girl. Whatever it is that you have to do, you need to get your strength back first.'

Her tone broached no reply. Éloïse took the bread and meat and bit into it. She found it delicious, and recalled that she had not eaten since the previous night. The nurse smiled to see her enjoying her food.

'That's better. At least now your legs might be able to hold you up.'

'Thank you! Thank you so much.'

Éloïse planted a kiss on the nurse's cheek, then quickly walked away before the old woman had time to stop her. She emerged from the crypt and took a deep breath. An old man, his heavy hand resting on a little girl's shoulder, spoke to her.

'Miss,' said the patriarch with a dignified air, 'my granddaughter and I wish to pray to the Black Virgin. Is this the way to her chapel?'

'Yes,' replied Éloïse, pushing open the door to the crypt. 'Turn right at the bottom of the stairs, and the corridor there will lead you to the holy well and the Black Virgin.'

'Thank you, Miss. May Our Lady bless you and your family.'

'May she hear your prayers and mine,' murmured Éloïse as she stood aside for the pilgrims.

Her heart heavy, she gently closed the door behind them and made her way out of the cathedral.

40

The room was cold. Galeran stared at the angel in the stained glass that hung above him. He had slept badly, and in his sleep the awful events of the past days had blurred with terrible nightmares. Now as he lay awake he realised how much he missed Audouard. He had somehow not been aware before the glazier's death of the strength of their friendship. And he thought now of Ausanne, who had spent the night behind the high walls of the Prévôté.

The knight shook himself from his reverie, put on a shirt and went out into the garden. There was a tub of water on the stone bench. Galeran plunged his head in and shook it vigorously. He dried himself off, then went to knock on Hermine's door. She opened it immediately, looking as though she had slept no better than the knight, and greeted him.

'You look pale, Hermine.'

'I'm fine. Come, knight, I shall make you something to eat.'

'You must join me for breakfast, Hermine.'

'I am not very hungry, Sir.'

'Nor am I. But eat we must, for we have a hard day ahead of us. Thiberge asked me to allow Audouard's body to remain in his atelier. His colleagues wanted to keep watch over him. I could not refuse him.'

'You did right, for my brother liked his men well.'

Galeran gave her a thick piece of rye bread spread with honey and a cup of mulled wine.

'Hermine, what are you going to do? This house belongs to the Bishop, and he will take it back now.'

'My God, I had not thought of that. What will happen to me?' said the old woman in a panic.

'Have you some friends here?'

'Yes, but . . . '

'But what?'

'I don't know . . . Perhaps I could ask Ausanne.'

'My dear Hermine . . . But how could you know? You spent yesterday in your room!'

'Something has happened to our dear Ausanne?'

'Yes.'

'She is . . . '

'No. But it might be better so, for the worst is yet to come. She is under lock and key in the Prévôté.'

'Tell me, Galeran,' she said softly.

'Ausanne is accused of and has confessed to poisoning the serving girl from the Rovin Vignon and killing Ogier the jeweller.'

'Calumny!' cried Hermine.

'She has admitted it publicly.'

Hermine shook her head in disbelief. Then she sat up straight and wiped away her tears.

'Can you tell me, knight, why a pious and devoted woman would do such a thing?'

'To protect someone else, I suppose,' said Galeran wearily. 'More I do not know. But what is it, my dear?'

Hermine had sprung to her feet and was rushing off to her room.

'I shall be right back!'

Out of breath and her hair more dishevelled than usual, Hermine re-emerged with Audouard's pouch.

'Here, this is for you. Audouard gave it to me the morning of his death.'

Galeran took the pouch and held it in his hand for a moment before opening it. Inside was a small parchment tied with a string. He rolled the document out on the table and began to slowly read the words his friend had written for him:

'By the grace of God, Galeran de Lesneven, my dearest friend, I shall be dead when you read this. Look in my chest and you shall find a roll of vellum and a blue gemstone. Take them for your own, they are my most precious belongings, they hold the secret of my colour! One day you shall pass them on to whomsoever you deem fit.

'You will also discover a purse, in which you will find a sum of money that will enable Hermine to live comfortably. Seek out Thiberge, and he will give you the keys to the house I bought from him in Bourg Muret. Look after my sister.

'As for the rest, the promise I made to you is sacred: Nivelon is the guilty one!

'May Our Lady shield you from all danger!

'Audouard, Master Glazier, in this month of May 1145, in the town of Chartres.'

Galeran stood silently for some time, then took up the parchment again and read aloud the paragraph concerning Hermine.

'You see, Hermine, your brother did not forget you.'

The woman nodded. Large tears rolled down her cheeks.

'I must go and see the master foreman this morning,' said the knight. 'I shall speak to him of this. You know I must soon leave Chartres. I have to be in Blois in a few days and I shall leave either tonight or tomorrow morning. If you are willing, I would like to entrust your affairs to a man in whom I have every confidence. He is a Breton like myself.'

'I trust in your choice and am happy to put my destiny in your hands as my brother wished.'

'Then I shall ask Robert le Breton to come and see you. He has the ear of the Bishop, and I shall ask him to ensure that you are not put out of this house before your new home in Bourg Muret is ready to receive you.'

There followed a long silence that was interspersed with the old woman's sobs.

'Thiberge de Soissons will have work on the cathedral stopped before midday, whereupon all the workers will pay homage to Audouard. A procession will then make its way to the collegiate church of Saint-André. Robert le Breton organised everything yesterday. I shall send one of Audouard's assistants to fetch you, and I shall wait for you at his atelier before the Angelus. Until then, I suggest you rest.'

'Very well, Sir. I promise I will be strong.'

'I have never doubted your courage, Hermine!' said the knight, kissing her on the cheek.

There was a knock on the door.

'Please go, knight, and see who it is,' pleaded Hermine. 'I am not expecting anyone, and I wish to see no one.'

'Go and rest. I shall see that no one disturbs you.'

Galeran flung open the door to find before him a very young woman with long russet plaits. She looked him up and down before speaking with a child's voice.

'Ausanne described you well, Chevalier Galeran! I am Éloïse, her sister. I must speak with you.'

'Not here, girl! Dame Hermine is tired, and I must go to the cathedral. We shall speak as we walk.'

He took the girl by the arm and marched off.

'What do you want from me, girl?'

'Ausanne liked you a lot. She said you were a good man.'

'I am in no mood for flattery. Tell me what you want.'

A little intimidated by the knight's severity, Éloïse swallowed and slowly began to explain her purpose.

'Three things. I want to see my sister again. I want you to explain what happened. And I want to understand.'

Galaeran sighed deeply.

'It is not for me explain all this to you. But one thing you must know – your sister killed an innocent child. For that heinous crime she must die!'

'That's not possible! You know that. Ausanne could never have done such a thing! Not my sister!'

'Yes, Éloïse. It was her. Of that, at least, I am sure,' said Galeran. 'What will your family do?'

'My parents are filled with fear and shame. The Provost came to tell us the news last night. He stayed a long time and he told us we should leave Chartres without delay.'

'I think he is right.'

'And why do you think that?' demanded Éloïse, shaking off the knight's arm and turning to face him.

'The people of Chartres will never forgive you for what your sister has done. I saw the crowd in front of the Prévôté yesterday, and I didn't like the look of them. The mob is like a rabid animal. Tell your parents to take the Provost's advice. They must leave quickly, and they must on no account go near the Vieux Fossés this afternoon!'

'My God!' cried the girl. 'You're not going to let her die such a dishonourable death!'

'Go home, there is nothing you can do!' growled Galeran.

'Help me at least see Ausanne one last time. I beg you!'

'I fear I will have to disappoint you, Éloïse. I think your sister wants to be alone, and, moreover, she needs the solace of religion more than your tears. She will require all the strength she can muster to face the gallows. So leave her in peace, and pray for her soul!'

'How dare you speak to me like that!'

'It was you who sought me out. But enough! Go home now and take care of your family.'

Galeran took the girl by the shoulders and softened his voice a little.

'I swear to you that if she were innocent, I would have battled all the soldiers in the world to free her!'

Éloïse lifted her eyes to the knight's face. She saw that Galeran was sincere and that her sister's condemnation was as painful to him as it was to herself.

'Forgive me, Sir. I shall do what you say and advise my parents to do the same. May the Black Virgin protect us!'

With that she gathered up the folds of her robe and ran off to join her family.

41

Groups of people had been forming in the streets of Chartres since the hanging had been announced. All in the town knew Ausanne. Some said she could not be guilty, others railed against her. She knew each one of them, she had been to their bedsides, brought their children into the world, administered potions, and even saved the lives of some of them.

But in one day her beauty had become baleful, her talent suspect and her remedies poisonous. Some began to ask if the phials she had left in people's homes might not be venomous. Cupboards were emptied and whatever Ausanne might have touched was thrown out.

Urchins threw stones at the shuttered windows of her little house. They climbed over the lattice fence to trample her vegetables and medicinal herbs and piss on her flower beds. A squad of soldiers from the Prévôté chased them away. The men had come to carry out part of the sentence passed on Ausanne. They were here to burn down her house.

They broke down the door with their axes, piled drapes, parchments, and furniture pell-mell in the middle of the room, and poured pitch over the floor. Then they marched out again, and one of them threw his torch back in through the fractured door.

The crowd that had gathered to watch the spectacle shouted with joy as fire engulfed the house. The roaring flames reached as far as the old apple trees in the garden. Soon there was nothing left of Ausanne's house but a pile of smoking ashes, which the men-at-arms scattered with furious kicks.

At the other end of town Robert le Breton made his way through a crowd that had gathered silently near the Prévôté, not hesitating to use his staff on any who failed to move aside. He arrived at the gate, where two men-at-arms stood imperturbably with their pikes crossed.

'Let me pass. I am here to see the Provost.'

The men recognised the cleric and raised their pikes to let

him through. The Provost had the previous evening refused to let the Breton see Ausanne, but now, after a brief audience, he granted permission. A guard escorted him to the room where she was being held. The solider unlocked the door and made as if to go into the room along with Robert.

'Leave us, my friend,' said the Breton. 'You may stay by the door outside.'

'But she is a murderess! The Provost said no one was to go in there without an escort.'

'She is a friend, and someone who has strayed from God! This is no longer a matter for men-at-arms but for the soldiers of Our Lord. Leave us. In the name of the Bishop, I order you!'

The soldier withdrew, anxious not to displease such an important figure. Robert turned slowly to face the prisoner.

Ausanne was on her feet by the empty fireplace, staring at the ashes. She did not turn her head.

'I have not changed my mind since yesterday.'

'Perhaps not, but I have. I cannot let you depart like this, my child.'

'Do not call me that. I have long since lost the innocence that goes with that word. And what a lovely term, depart! Do you think I am going to let those fools drag me to the gallows?'

'What do you mean, Ausanne?'

'Almost everyone here owes me their life,' she said, ignoring his question. 'Even you, if I remember correctly. I saved you. Me, the poor, little weaver! Without me you would now be with this God you venerate, this God who has long since abandoned me!'

Her face white with anger, Ausanne turned to face the priest. Robert moved back, as though this almost palpable hatred had dealt him a blow.

'You blaspheme, Ausanne! Do not think you possess a power that only God can have.'

'God needed me to treat purulent wounds, to open stomachs, banish tumours, deliver babies that were dying in their mothers' wombs . . . '

Robert grabbed her by the arm.

'Stop! You are playing with the Devil! You will be damned for eternity if you do not repent.'

'I know it, Sir. And it pleases me better than to beg God to spare me.'

'Repent, Ausanne. There is still time.'

'What can I fear? What can there be that is worse than life on this earth? Why should I want the pardon of Him who would let me be dragged to the gallows, who cruelly takes away the life He supposedly has given me?'

Robert le Breton lowered his eyes.

'May God forgive you, Ausanne, as I do,' he murmured.

'You do not understand, Sir. I am already dead! Neither you nor God nor the Devil can do anything for me now.'

The priest looked at her as though to etch on his memory the terrible image of this face deformed by hatred and fear. Then he turned and left the room without a word.

Ausanne flung herself at the door as it closed behind him, and thumped it with her fists until they drew blood.

'Come back! Don't leave me here alone! Come back!'

Outside on the street the shouts of the crowd seemed to echo Ausanne's plea.

'Death to the witch!' came the cries. 'Death to the cursed redhead! Death to the poisoner!'

The mob began to stamp their feet faster and faster, making the walls and the floor of the Prévôté shake.

42

At the cathedral the atmosphere was no better. Audouard was dead, and a day's work had been lost due to the storm.

Almost seven hundred workers had gathered around a platform on which stood the canons and the master foreman. The masons and the stonecutters were demanding compensation for the lost day's work. The master glaziers were refusing to return to the building, some out of respect for Audouard, others out of fear.

Only Thiberge de Soissons remained calm. He stood above his workers, pensively stroking his short beard. He struck the ground with the long staff that was a symbol of his authority, and the workers fell silent.

'You have given of your best, and Our Lady, who watches us, loves you all the more for this. She is allowing us to build . . . Have you forgotten,' this giant of a man suddenly growled, 'that she is allowing us to build a house for her, a house of God?'

A murmur ran through the crowd.

'Do we have to go and fetch other men, men who will be proud to build her house?'

Cries of protest rose up.

'Must I carry on alone with the construction of this house of God? Nothing will stop me. Before your eyes, you who deny Our Lady and renege on your word, I shall put stone upon stone to raise up this house! Where are the men that I chose, the men who chose me?'

Galeran, who had mingled with the workers, admired Thiberge's oratorical talent. He was not only a fine architect, but also a leader who could fill men's hearts with valour as he led them into combat. He sensed that the master foreman had won this battle and that the workers would now return to their labour. The carpenters, led by the old Breton, were already moving back inside the building.

Thiberge de Soissons now stared silently at the crowd, his

hands resting on his cane. The workers began to disperse, and soon there was no one to return his gaze. He climbed down from the platform along with the canons.

'Ah, Chevalier Galeran!' he said, catching sight of the knight. 'Come, I beg you. Follow me to my workroom. We shall have more peace there.'

Galeran fell in beside him, but struggled to keep up with the man's long strides. When they came to a stone house beside the cathedral, the architect pushed open its door and stood aside to let the knight go in first. Even in Saint-Denis Galeran had never penetrated the architects' offices, wherein the plans for the house of God were drawn up.

All drawings and models for the cathedral were generated in this vast room. On the paved floor the architect would make life-size drawings with the aid of compass or set square. At the side of the room were piles of wooden models of ogives, mullions, joists and brackets. Light filtered in through the open shutters of the windows.

Thiberge had had to force the Bishop's hand a little to be granted his famous atelier. He argued that to protect against inclement weather and the wind that was all too frequent a visitor to this hilltop site, the house must be built in stone and have solid roofing. The Bishop was somewhat distressed by the cost, but in the end gave in.

'Take a seat,' said Thiberge as he led Galeran to a bench in a corner of the room. 'Let us come straight to the point. Audouard said you were a perceptive man and I need your help. This disorder cannot go on! The workers are so restless, particularly with this sorry execution. And if I lose any more men . . . '

Galeran waited for the architect to continue, but Thiberge said nothing more for a while. He stared, tight-lipped, at the ground for what seemed like minutes. Then he burst brutally into speech.

'Audouard thought he knew who the guilty one was, and it was for that reason that he perished!' he exclaimed, his face purple with anguish.

'I could have saved his life if I had made him tell me,' he went on. 'But you know how he was. Stubborn as a mule! He wanted to do things his way. He did, however, tell me after Jérôme's death that he might share his suspicions with you.'

'Who do you think he had in mind?'

Galeran's voice had an almost metallic edge.

'By my faith, I do not know,' answered Thiberge. 'Perhaps he spoke to Enguerrand about it. They had an odd relationship, those two. Sometimes the best of friends, sometimes the bitterest enemies. Enguerrand even told me he thought Audouard might be the cause of all this!'

'He accused Audouard?'

'Oh, he didn't accuse him of murder, but he did say that he was to blame. But then I have to admit that Enguerrand is a little deranged. I often have the impression that some folly has possessed him.'

'Is it not dangerous to employ such a man here?'

'Yes, but as a sculptor he surpasses even Gislebertus d'Autun! I have never in my life met a man with such talent. Have you seen his work?'

'Certainly. Téobald showed me what he did at the Royal Portal.'

'Téobald the carpenter?'

'The very same.'

'The Royal Portal is the most complete of his works here. But to truly know his work you must go to the south tower. There he is sculpting a figure . . . But you will understand when you see it.'

'I must meet this Enguerrand. I have heard so much about him since I arrived in Chartres. I have seen his creations in stone, but not the man himself. He is like a phantom. I sometimes wonder does he exist at all. Where may I find him?'

'At this hour he will most certainly be working on the statue I told you about.'

'Can one of your men take me there?'

'Of course. Brunel will go with you. He knows Notre Dame almost as well as myself. Yet I have not seen Enguerrand since Audouard's death. It might be dangerous to seek him out now, for his mind may be rattled by the loss of his friend. Do you want me to send two or three sturdy workers with you?'

'You think that would be necessary? No. I shall go alone. We should fear more for him than for me.'

The master foreman called Brunel away from his work at one of the tables. The young man, who could not have been older than fourteen, ran over to his master.

'What is your command?'

'Take the knight to the place where Enguerrand works, in the south tower. Be careful, both of you, and may Our Lady watch over you.'

'Thank you, Thiberge. But two more things: Audouard spoke to me of a house he bought from you in Bourg Muret . . . '

'That's right. He had some money put aside and he wanted to settle down here in Chartres, given the volume of work that remained to be done. And he had set up a glassworks with a companion, and it was bringing in some money. When I mentioned that I owned a house in Bourg Muret that I didn't use, he asked me to sell it to him. We sealed the deal last month.'

'So everything was in order between you? I ask you that because Audouard's last wishes were that I should look after his sister. I am to meet Dame Hermine at the funeral, and it would be good if you were to seek her out there and give her the keys to the house.'

'That I will do. And the second question?'

'Who is Nivelon?'

The master foreman looked confused.

'Is he supposed to be someone working here?'

'I think so.'

'Well, I know all the master craftsmen personally and there is no Nivelon among them. But as for the workers . . . There are almost a thousand labourers and carters, five hundred masons, twenty carpenters and smiths, a hundred apprentice stonecutters and glaziers. The list is long. I can find out if there is a Nivelon there somewhere, but it will take some time.'

'I would be grateful if you could. It might prevent another death.'

'May I ask where you got this name from?'

'From the words of a dead man. From Audouard.'

'And he said no more?'

'Alas, no.'

'Very well. And you, stop hopping from one leg to the other,' said Thiberge to young Brunel. 'Take the knight where he wants to go. You are responsible for his security on the scaffolding. And you must obey him as you do me!'

'Very well, master,' replied the young worker.

43

The two men walked briskly towards the south tower. They took the spiral staircase and when they were near the top the young man jumped nimbly onto the rungs of a ladder that hung high over the vast emptiness of the cathedral. The knight looked down into the abyss for a moment before following his guide across to the platform where he now stood and waited.

'Where are we going, Brunel? Does this man work at the very top of the cathedral?'

'Oh yes, Sir. Enguerrand works three platforms higher up. We have to go up there,' he said, pointing to a series of frail-looking ladders that led from one level to the next.

'Let us go, then. But stop before you reach his platform. I want to see him alone.'

'Yes, Sir.'

They continued their climb. The higher they got, the fewer workers they encountered. The master stonecutter was the only one who worked so high up and in such an exposed place. There were no safety rails at this height. Through the rungs of the ladder the men working on the ground looked like insects.

'I shall wait for you here,' said Brunel. 'He should be just above you now.'

'Thank you.'

Galeran took out a dagger, placed it between his teeth and began his ascent. But his caution was unnecessary, for once again the bird had fled its nest. There was no one on the platform. An unfinished sculpture filled one corner, a chisel resting on it, and on the ground lay an open bag. The man must have heard them coming. Galeran looked around to see how he might have got away. The only exit route he could see was along a very narrow cornice, below which there was nothing but the distant ground.

The knight sheathed his dagger and looked at the sculpture. He suddenly understood Thiberge's enigmatic words.

Enguerrand had hewn from the stone a mythical creature, its human head perched on a bird's body. He had carefully sculpted eyes in which he had pierced large pupils. The stone beast stared out over the town, its mouth twisted in a grimace. Its wings were half-spread as though it were about to take flight, and its claws gripped the flesh of the cathedral. Was it his own portrait that the man had carved in the rock? Galeran knelt down and placed the palm of his hand on the creature's face. He pulled it back immediately, his skin marked with a burn that could not be blamed on the sun. It was with a troubled face that Galeran climbed back down the ladder to Brunel.

'Did you see him, Sir?'

'No. But he is no man, he is a Devil, this Enguerrand! May Our Lady forgive me! Let us go, Brunel, I have seen enough.'

They went their separate ways when they arrived back on the ground.

'Tell your master that I have gone to talk to Dame Hermine at Audouard's atelier,' said the knight. 'Tell him also that I now understand what he meant.'

44

Hermine, dressed entirely in brown, was already at the atelier. She had not had the patience to wait for someone to fetch her from her home. Her brother's workers, who knew her well, had sat her down and given her a cup of wine.

When Galeran arrived she got shakily to her feet. The knight took her by the arm and led her to the Royal Portal. The twenty-strong funeral procession soon arrived. The men, singing as they walked, were led by Robert le Breton. In order that his companions could pay homage to him, the litter bearing Audouard's body was placed beneath the window portraying the Jesse tree. The glaziers placed over the bier a silk cloth dyed the blue Audouard had loved. In the scaffolding the workers ceased their work and briefly clapped as a mark of their respect. Then silence fell over the cathedral.

Thiberge de Soissons placed Audouard's satchel on the bier. It was a tradition that no master craftsman should enter the afterlife without his tools. Thiberge then went to offer his condolences to Hermine, who was crying quietly into her handkerchief. Frère Gacé was among the mourners and he also now came to offer words of sympathy to Hermine.

Galeran discreetly sought out Robert le Breton to ask him to speak with Hermine. The priest's mind was still full of the events of his interview with Ausanne, and he began to talk of this. But he quickly stopped when he saw Galeran's face darken. The knight was only too aware that Ausanne's agony was nearing.

The procession, now swollen to some fifty people, chanted as it marched off to follow the Eure towards the church of Saint-André where Audouard was to be inhumed.

Thiberge ordered the men to finish working as a mark of respect for their dead colleague. And, as a means of regaining their confidence, he also told them they would be paid for a full day. Many of the workers tagged along behind the funeral procession, as much to see the rare spectacle of a public execution as to honour the dead man.

Galeran noted that the cortège was taking almost exactly the same route he had followed five days previously when he arrived in the town. Death had, now as often before, completed the circle.

Bishop Geoffroy de Lèves arrived with a dozen canons in the middle of the ceremony to pay homage to the glazier. His clergymen were the first to shovel earth onto the blue silk at the bottom of the grave.

45

Not far away, near Vieux Fossés, a rope had been placed on the oak tree that the people of Chartres used for their gallows. The noose hung down from a sturdy branch. A stepladder was in place to allow Ausanne to climb up to face her agony. The workmen, pleased with their handiwork, stood about and exchanged macabre jokes. Some people had already gathered for the hanging and sat playing dice on the grass as they waited. Two dark figures, their hoods drawn up over their heads, stood nearby in the shade of the trees.

An impatient crowd was already moving through the streets of the town towards Porte Guillaume to attend the poisoner's execution. In the upper town the mob's mood was ugly.

The Provost feared the crowd might try to seize Ausanne and dispense its own form of justice. He had the young woman sent for. A tumbril stood ready in the courtyard, the horses were harnessed, and the soldiers armed and ready to leave.

'Sir Provost, come quickly!'

'What is it now? Aren't you man enough to escort a woman on your own?'

'Come! Come and see!' said the soldier, running off back towards Ausanne's improvised cell.

The Provost, sensing more misfortune, also began to run.

The soldier who had helped Ausanne prepare for her death had granted her request that she be allowed to keep the two russet plaits he had cut from her head. When he left her she had tied them together to make a sort of rope, then placed a bench on top of the table, tied the rope to the bars of the high window, and hanged herself. Her beauty now gone, her eyes bulging, blood flowing from her mouth and nose, Ausanne had chosen to damn herself a second time.

The Provost gave a cry of rage.

'Get her down from there, by God! Get her down!'

Some men-at-arms arrived and helped the soldier slide the body down onto the ground.

The crowd outside kept up its din, calling for blood.

'What am I going to do now?' roared the Provost. 'They want their hanging. Well, I'll give it to them! Take her away!'

'But . . . '

'You two take her to the tumbril. And you, fetch the carpenter.'

'The carpenter?'

'Yes, and sharp!'

Two men-at-arms took up Ausanne's body and carried it out into the courtyard. The carpenter, an old soldier with a scarred face, soon arrived.

'Right, you, find me some planks. I want the body to stand up straight in the cart.'

'Yes, Sir,' said the carpenter.

A quarter of an hour later Ausanne's body was tied to a sort of cross hoisted upright on the tumbril. One of the men-at-arms, his heart sickened at the sight, had wiped the coagulated blood from the physician's face and placed a piece of cloth around the mouth that had been deformed by pain. The Provost also ordered a rag to be placed around her neck to hide the blue mark of the rope, and himself tied her head to the post so that it would not sway as the cart moved over the cobblestones. Ausanne's lifeless eyes stared straight ahead. Her red hair, now cut short, was the only colour in this bloodless body.

Four men-at-arms took their places on the tumbril. The crowd outside stamped its feet impatiently. The soldiers' hearts were in their boots. They drew their swords when the Provost ordered the gates to be opened. A buzz of excitement ran through the mob when the cart emerged, escorted by a dozen cavalrymen and preceded by the Provost himself. Pikemen pushed people aside to clear the path.

'So you want to see the poisoner hanged?' cried the Provost.

The crowd responded with a delirious roar.

'Then go to the gallows and let us through here.'

The Provost had played the mob correctly, and it now opened up to let the tumbril through.

'Go past the cathedral!' shouted the Provost to the man holding the reins. 'Everyone must see her!'

The procession did a tour of Notre Dame, the horsemen not hesitating to distribute blows with their maces if a spectator got too close. The Provost continued to ride at the front, spurring on his mount with a rush.

Enguerrand stood in the shade of the tower. The tall, thin figure had watched Audouard's funeral procession from his lofty perch, and had then sat down as though exhausted. His scarred face was blue from the cold, and dark rings hung under his eyes.

He stood up again, gripping the guardrail, and stared, transfixed, at a strange procession that had just arrived at the Royal Portal and begun to snake its way around the cathedral. At the sight of the crucified figure of Ausanne, Enguerrand gave a cry like that of a wounded animal and buried his face in his hands. Then, still screaming as though in pain, he rushed back towards his shelter high above the world of men.

46

The day might have taken a less tragic course had the weather been fine. But the sky was heavy and painted black, and lightning flickered over the far bank of the river. Rumbles of thunder added to the trepidation of a crowd already inflamed by heat and wine. Workers from Notre Dame had joined the goliards and animal skinners among the rabble. The men-at-arms had dealt out and received many blows to clear a path through Porte Guillaume. The road from there to the gallows was clear, and the driver of the tumbril whipped his horses to a gallop. The Provost and his men followed closely behind in a cloud of dust.

When they arrived at the gallows the Provost shouted at his escort to form a circle round the hundred-year-old tree. The spectators, who had been lying on the grass as they waited for the show to begin, jumped to their feet.

Galeran arrived on horseback with Robert le Breton, dismounted and marched up to the Provost.

'What have you done?' he cried, staring at Ausanne's trussed and gagged body.

'Oh, calm yourself, Sir! She did it herself. My men found her hanged in her cell.'

'So what is this masquerade?' exclaimed Robert le Breton. 'You are not planning to . . . '

'Take her down immediately!' said Galeran, reaching for his sword.

The crowd was now flooding onto the esplanade. Peasants and townsfolk, poor and rich, merchants and artisans massed around the soldiers. The glint of a pitchfork or an axe could be glimpsed here and there. Harlots spitting insults hitched up their dresses to provoke the men-at-arms.

A detachment of archers requested by the Provost took up position opposite the crowd. They nocked their arrows and made ready to fire.

'We are wasting precious time!' screamed the Provost. 'Move

aside! If you want to know why, just take a look at this lovely lot. If I deprive them of their hanging, they will massacre my soldiers, and maybe even attack the Vicomte or the Bishop!'

Galeran and Robert le Breton exchanged glances.

'Must we permit this act of infamy?' asked the priest.

'I think we no longer have the choice,' replied the knight, turning, still gripping the handle of his sword, to look at the crowd.

Already a soldier had untied the body and removed the cloth that hid the marks of the suicide. The Provost gave a sign and the man held the body up above him to display it for the crowd, then threw it over his shoulders and climbed down from the tumbril. The mob howled in horror, then fell silent as it waited for the final act.

The soldiers moved aside. The inert body was hoisted up the stepladder, whereupon two men lifted it up to the rope. One of them placed the noose around Ausanne's bruised neck. The stepladder was kicked violently aside and the body was left hanging for the second time like a puppet on a string.

Suddenly from the crowd came the plaintive sobs of a child that grew slowly into an almost inhuman cry, a heart-rending scream that stopped as abruptly as it had begun. The sound came from Éloïse's lips. She and Benoît had mingled with the crowd, and now she could no longer contain her horror at the sight of her sister's degradation. She fell to her knees and her hood slipped off her head to reveal her long, red plaits. All eyes turned to this girl who now sat crying and wringing her hands. The crowd drew back as though she were stricken with plague.

'Kill the redhead!' an old hag suddenly screamed.

'Death to the murderess!' came another cry.

'Death! Death!' chanted the crowd, which now hoped to see a living person suffer after watching a dead one hang.

Benoît brandished a stick and managed to keep at bay two frenzied women who tried to set upon his sister.

'Come on, you cowards! Touch my sister and I'll kill you!'

'He's another one of them! Kill them both! After the beasts! We want blood!'

Éloïse was still on her knees behind her brother. Pale as

death, she swung her body back and forwards and prayed to be taken from this place.

Women, their children in tow, jostled for a better view. Benoît stared defiantly at the crowd around him. He saw faces he had once known as friendly that were now twisted with hatred. The mob moved in closer and closer, and stones began to rain down on the brother and sister.

'Get back! Not another inch!' a powerful voice suddenly called out.

Galeran strode through the crowd, striking any who did not move quickly enough with the flat edge of his sword, and took up position beside Benoît.

'Whoever touches a hair on these children's heads,' warned the knight, 'by my faith, I shall cut him in two!'

The crowd moved back, as though to catch its breath.

'Pick up your sister,' Galeran ordered Benoît. 'I shall whistle for my horse, and when he comes you two get on him and get out of here. If you don't you are dead! They want blood!'

'Yes, Sir,' replied the boy.

The crowd was moving in again.

'We have nothing against you, Sir,' said a man at the front of the mob.

'Death!' cried the women. 'Hang them! Skin the fiends!'

A stone struck Éloïse on the shoulder. The knight whistled for Quolibet who came whinnying and rearing through the rabble. He then lashed out at two animal skinners who advanced on him brandishing their meat hooks. Robert le Breton, who had come to the knight's aid, struck down a third.

'I thank you. Look to your right!' Galeran cried.

The knight knocked over a robust matron who tried to get to the children. Galeran, the Breton and Benoît formed a circle around Éloïse as she rose unsteadily to her feet. Quolibet was at hand now, his nostrils flaring, rearing up and kicking out each time the crowd approached.

'Benoît, put her on the horse and go!' thundered Galeran.

Robert le Breton was fighting like a man possessed, enthusiastically smashing the skulls of sinners. A man in a monk's habit, whom Galeran did not recognise, came to fight at their side.

Attacked by two men with clubs, the knight raised up his sword and charged with a great cry. His assailants, more used to drunken brawls than proper combat, immediately took flight. Galeran turned around in time to dodge the blow of an axe. He jumped to one side and sliced the attacker's hams with his sword. The man screamed in pain and fell to the ground.

In just a few minutes the esplanade had become a battlefield. But the men-at-arms did not move from their position around the gallows. They awaited a sign from the Provost, a sign which still did not come. Éloïse had by now climbed up on the horse's back. Benoît climbed up behind her, held his sister tight against him, and began to manoeuvre the beast through the crowd. But a stone caught him on the side of the head, and he slumped back on the saddle and fell to the ground, dragging Éloïse with him.

The monk ran towards the children but an old peasant knifed him as he passed and he fell at his assailant's feet.

Now only Galeran and Robert le Breton were still standing, cutting and slashing as best they could.

'If the Provost does not intervene soon, he will have our deaths on his conscience, never mind those of the poor fools we are fighting,' thought the knight.

Suddenly the rabble began to move back. The tocsin of Notre Dame had rung out, and was soon echoed by the bells in all the churches in the town. Abandoning their wounded, the crowd surged back towards Porte Guillaume. A column of black smoke had been spotted near Notre Dame.

Galeran ran towards the two children. Benoît was sitting up on the ground. His wounds were minor but his head was still sore from the blows he had received. Éloïse, seeing that her brother did not need her, went towards the monk who lay motionless on the ground. Galeran helped her turn him over and was surprised to see that before him lay Frère Gacé. A broken blade was lodged in his shoulder.

'What's happening?' muttered the monk as he opened his eyes.

Galeran cut open his habit to examine the wound. He saw that the blade had not gone in far.

'Be still, brother,' he said. 'I must remove the blade before I bandage you.'

'Well, get it over with then,' said the monk, gritting his teeth.

'It might be better if you didn't watch,' said the knight, swiftly pulling out the broken knife.

Gacé barely twitched as the blade came out, and he was soon sitting up.

'I am no milksop!' he protested.

'Absolutely not,' replied Galeran, smiling as he wiped away the monk's blood with a piece of cloth Éloïse gave him. 'But you are a very agreeable patient!'

Éloïse tore some more strips from her petticoat with which Galeran wrapped a tight bandage around Gacé's arm and shoulder.

A few yards away the Provost argued bitterly with Robert le Breton. He had already sent his archers back to town and was set to leave himself.

'I was about to step in,' he said, 'but you didn't give me enough time.'

'I think you had not the slightest intention of intervening,' retorted the priest. 'But let us be charitable . . . '

'It all happened so quickly. And now a fire!' said an embarrassed Provost. 'I must get back to town. Please excuse me.'

He gave his men a sign to follow him, then rode off.

47

Thick black smoke rose up above Notre Dame cathedral. Téobald-the-carpenter's men, who had stayed behind to drink their extra wages in a tavern, were the first to spot the fire. They sounded the alarm and rushed to the sanctuary, where the sky was dark with smoke.

But suddenly there was a violent gust of wind that might have come from a hot oven, and the clouds burst open and rain poured down and drowned the fire.

The people of Chartres were delivered from their nightmare. Some fell to their knees to thank God for the miracle. They laughed and weeped as though they knew the fire was a warning to them for their impiety and excess.

It was some time before the workers reached the platform high up in one of the towers where the fire had begun. The rain had smothered the flames before they could reach the beams of the spire. The men found the burned body of Enguerrand hanging over the edge of the platform. They were about to climb up to it when what remained of the scaffolding inside the tower collapsed, bringing down with it the charred bones of the sculptor. Some of the men thought Enguerrand had accidentally set his clothes alight and thus started the fire. Others, more perceptive, believed he had taken his own life. But they said nothing, not daring to make public this terrible accusation.

48

Galeran stood and stared through the rain that shrouded the ghostly little form swinging gently from the gallows.

'There is no art to read men's minds or hearts,' Robert le Breton said softly, placing his hand on the knight's shoulder. 'I promise I shall do what I can to get her a decent grave.'

Galeran nodded, and turned to look the priest in the eye.

'By my faith, I know not how to thank you. You fought like a lion at my side. You are a true friend!'

'When justice guides my hand, I no longer know my strength!' said Robert, pleased at the knight's words.

He looked around him at the bodies littering the esplanade.

'Let the dead bury the dead, and let us take care of the living.'

'Let us begin with these children,' said Galeran, pointing to Éloïse and Benoît, who sat huddled together on the grass and shivered in the rain. 'We must get them somewhere safe.'

'I'll take charge of them,' said Robert le Breton. 'I shall bring them to my house on Rue de la Bretonnerie.'

'Take my horse. There is room for all three of you. I shall see to Frère Gacé.'

'How is he?'

'Not too bad. The wound was not deep. But take care that no one sees the red of the children's hair, for it has caused enough misfortunes for one day.'

Then he spoke to Benoît, his voice grave.

'Benoît, your family must leave Chartres without delay. Robert le Breton will help you.'

'Yes, Sir.'

'Today you fought like a man. Better even than many a man!'

The boy blushed, but Galeran had already turned to Gacé. The monk was resting on a tree stump, clearly in great pain. The rain had stopped and heat rose from the soaked earth. Gacé turned his dulled eyes to the knight.

'Knight, I have a story to tell you. And I must tell it, for there are perhaps other lives to be saves, and other souls in torment.'

They sat face to face in the now empty battlefield, and behind them Ausanne's body continued its solitary jig on the tree. The bloodstain on the monk's shoulder grew slowly larger.

'I always knew there was something more,' said the knight sadly. 'But you can tell me when we have left this place.'

Galeran helped him to his feet, slipping an arm round his considerable girth.

'Where are you taking me, knight?'

'To Dame Hermine. You're not strong enough to return to the sanatorium.'

They soon arrived at Audouard's house. Silence had fallen over the town. The people of Chartres were indoors, licking their wounds and nursing their wine and their shame.

49

Dame Hermine opened the door and gave a little cry when she saw the state they were in.

'What on earth has happened? Come in, come in, Frère Gacé. And you, Chevalier Galeran. Take off those wet clothes and get yourselves dried off. What happened?'

'My dear Hermine, it is a long story. Tell me how you are,' said the knight, affectionately taking her hands in his own.

'It was a hard day for me. I prayed much, and then the Lord allowed me a deep sleep. Your knock woke me.'

'Well then, you must return to your bed,' said Galeran. 'I shall tend to Frère Gacé.'

'I shall not refuse. There is some broth in the pantry, and some meat by the hearth. This poor monk must eat well to regain his strength.'

Galeran led her to her room, and gave her a tender kiss as he left her. Frère Gacé took off his habit and the knight washed the monk's wound and put on a fresh dressing. Then they sat down with two steaming bowls of broth and two pewter goblets of wine. They smiled at each other across the table.

'We look like we've been shipwrecked!' laughed Galeran.

But the monk's face darkened.

'That is truer than you might think,' he murmured.

'So, speak, Frère Gacé,' said the knight.

'The story begins eleven years ago, in 1134.'

He stopped, overcome with emotion. Galeran looked at his scarred and haggard face and suddenly realised the man was probably not much older than thirty.

'Go on, brother,' he said gently. 'Too many have already died because of this silence.'

'There were four of us,' said the monk. 'There were Jérôme and Nivelon, both young and passionate, and there were Audouard and myself. We were a little older than the others.'

'Audouard?' queried the knight.

'You see, we were a little band,' continued Gacé, as though

he had not heard the question. 'By day we worked. But by night things were different. We became wastrels, goliards, as they call them. We drank, we forced ourselves upon any girl who had the misfortune to fall into our hands. We had knife fights with other goliards. The Provost's men would pick up the dead and injured in the morning. The Devil was our accomplice, and the streets of Chartres a perfect setting for our crimes.'

The monk broke off to take a swig of wine.

'Audouard was the oldest of the four. He must have been about twenty-three at the time, and was the favourite pupil of a renowned glazier. And Ausanne was a girl like no other. She had promised herself to Nivelon, but everyone wanted her. Including Audouard, who did all he could to please her. But she had eyes for one man only, and that man was that unfortunate fool Nivelon.

'It was the fifth of September 1134, and I thought it was the Apocalypse! I saw the sky bright with flames. Perhaps God burned Chartres because he was sick of our debauchery and our crimes. The summer had been hot, too hot . . . '

Gacé fell silent, lost in his thoughts. Galeran watched him in fascination.

'The day began with a strange smell,' the monk went on. 'One of those smells you recognise but you cannot name. Then the tocsin of Notre Dame began to ring, as it did today, and was followed by all the bells in the town. But the alarm came too late, for the town was already ablaze. From the fields around Chartres the flames could be seen reaching up into the sky. The blaze leaped from one roof to another, quickly reducing the wattle-and-daub houses to ashes. The streets became unbearably hot, and a thick cloud of smoke enveloped the hill.

'The townsfolk at first battled the fire. As soon as the bell rang they began heaving buckets of water up from the river. Men, women, children, old folk all tried to save their homes. But the heat was too much, and soon everyone beat a retreat. The blaze took the town area by area.

'Panic set in among the people as they flooded towards the gates, trampling anyone who stood in their way. Columns of black smoke billowed up into the cloudless sky. In the plain surrounding the town it is said that pilgrims, travellers and peasants fell to their knees to beg God to spare them. I was near the Hôtel-Dieu when it caught fire. We naïvely thought we could save the building. I helped my companions to carry up water. A long line of men, women and children, their faces blackened by smoke, struggled elbow to elbow. To breathe we had to suck the boiling air slowly as though through a reed. I can still see Nivelon next to me, his face filthy, his long hair held back with a headscarf, passing a bucket on to Jérôme, who was next to Audouard. It was at that moment that the building collapsed with a sinister roar, and the hundred or so of the infirm inside went to their graves without a cry.'

Gacé stopped to catch his breath, and when he went on it was in such a low voice that Galeran had to lean forward to hear.

'When the smoke cleared the first thing I saw was a woman's hand poking out of the rubble. The fire had won! They were all dead. Or at least that is what I thought. And I alone was cursed enough to stay alive! Then the porch and the old tower went up. I think I cried out, but what I heard was not my own voice but a terrible scream that seemed to be answering my cry. Chartres was screaming, the town was a prisoner to the blaze, it faced ordeal by fire. Torrents of smoke poured upwards into the sky, and ash and soot covered the ground. The fire could now be several leagues away.

'Chartres was dying, and I stood and watched it perish. The houses belonging to the canons collapsed. Only the basilica was spared God's wrath. A crowd of people, trapped by the flames, took refuge there and prayed for the Lord to forgive them their sins!

'That day I made a vow to dedicate my life to the poor if God saved Notre Dame, my beloved basilica, now blackened with ash and full of the song of desperate men. I, like those around me, knelt and repented.'

With that the monk fell silent.

'Perhaps now you will tell me the rest of the story,' said Galeran after some time.

'What more do you wish to know?' replied Gacé, his voice trembling.

'All the years that have passed have served only to change the appearances of these men who fled justice!'

The monk nodded his head. 'You have guessed the truth.'

'How did the fire start? How many of the dead have come to you in your dreams to accuse you?'

'No!' cried Gacé. 'It was not me! Be quiet, by God, and I shall tell you all. That night Audouard had told Nivelon of his plans to marry Ausanne. Audouard was hoping that because he was older than his rival and had some money put aside, her parents would favour him. But Nivelon flew into a rage. Jérôme and I had to hold them apart. We brought them to a tavern to try and calm them down. They emptied a small barrel between them and then Audouard took his leave. He even shook Nivelon by the hand as he went. It was that night that the house where Audouard and myself were lodging caught fire. We should have been in our beds at the time, but we weren't, for we had gone down to the river to drink more wine and had fallen asleep there!'

'Let me tell the rest, Gacé. Nivelon wanted only to kill his rival, but things got out of control! And then he saw you, as though by some miracle, appear at his side to fight the flames. I imagine that, like Audouard, he fled Chartres that day. And many years later the two men met again in the same town. Everything would have been forgotten had the pair not made the regrettable decision to return to Notre Dame!'

'There was Ausanne . . . ' murmured the monk.

'Yes, Ausanne, whom that diabolical lover possessed once again! A lover for whom she damned herself not once but twice! The lover who killed old Ogier. The lover who pushed Jérôme to his death, the lover who finally killed his eternal rival, my friend Audouard, and destroyed his creation!'

'My God! You think Nivelon . . . '

'Yes, I do. I must find this man.'

'You have also guessed that . . . '

'That Enguerrand and Nivelon are one and same. Yes, Gacé, and I knew it when I saw one of the statues on the Royal Portal. Nivelon gave Queen Bathsheba Ausanne's face!'

Gacé's distress was painful to behold. A heavy silence lay between the two men, punctuated by the monk's rapid breath.

'But tell me, knight, why would Nivelon suddenly start all this after ten years of silence? Why should we think that he has done nothing all this time? He is a perverted creature who takes pleasure in evil deeds. He may well have committed many a cruel and immoral act. Audouard suspected as much, and thought he was behind the accidents at the cathedral. But the poor man dared admit it neither to himself nor to me!'

'But to kill with his own hand!'

'Who knows? Chance had it that an old jeweller caught a chill as he forded a river and had to stay in his room till he recovered. And chance had it that the man's window looked directly onto the cathedral. Ogier must have seen Nivelon at some misdeed. Audouard told me that the Friday before the jeweller died a carpenter was almost killed in one of the towers. Did Ogier see Nivelon that day? In any case, he made the mistake of confiding in Ausanne, who ran to tell her devilish lover.'

Gacé shook his head.

'The rest is clear. But I cannot judge them. Have not I too been a criminal?'

'I do not judge either, brother. But if the man is not stopped the next victim could well be you.'

'Me?'

'You are the only one left who knows. You are the last of the five still living! But go and rest now. I see you are weary. I shall go and seek out the murderer.'

The knight had gone but a few paces along the street when he met with some Breton workers who told him that the sculptor had died the same fiery death that he had inflicted on his many victims.

50

The Rovin Vignon was closed. The little terrace under the wooden canopy was deserted, and boards were nailed across the door and windows. Women crossed themselves as they passed, and hurried on their way. Men looked guiltily away.

Galeran had come to look upon the abandoned tavern as he left Chartres. The jeweller, Jehan, La Doëtte – all had lived there, had loved and hated there, and all had come to an unjust end. Galeran pictured the little serving girl, and saw again the hard-headed innkeeper lean against the door and admiringly watch the slender figure of his veiled wife walk up the street in her green dress.

'The inn is for sale if you're interested, knight!'

Galeran turned to see a man with the air of a solid burgher about him.

'Do we know each other, Sir?' he snapped.

'No, but we can quickly change that! I am Master Giffard and a man of good repute. As for you, Sir, please forgive my indiscretion, but I have had many an occasion these last few days to admire your composure and your courage!'

The men had, without noticing, begun to make their way along the street as they talked. Giffard was a portly chap of some fifty years, with a pleasant demeanour and a spring in his step.

'I knew Jehan de Toulouse well, you know. For thirty years now I have traded with the Castilians and the Moors of Spain. Jehan owned an inn called Le Bon Saint Jacques in Saint-Gaudens, on the road to Compostela near the source of the Garonne river. He made his fortune on the back of all the pilgrims and clergymen passing through. I often stopped off there.

'Jehan made Mahaut's acquaintance in a bawdy house in the town. He fell for her badly and soon had but one aim in life, and that was to reform the sinful woman. He sold off his tavern for a very tidy sum and set up shop here in Chartres, Mahaut's home town.'

The men had by now arrived at Mallon the goldsmith's shop. Master Giffard gave the knight a mischievous look.

'Sir, I have to collect an order I placed with Mallon. He's made a gold chain for my wife and silver buckles for my daughters' shoes. Would you like to come in with me?'

Galeran hesitated.

'Come, Sir,' insisted his companion. 'There might be something here that interests you.'

The goldsmith stood up from his workbench when he saw them come in.

'I greet you, good sirs,' he said with a bow. 'Master Giffard, your order is ready. Come and inspect it, and we shall then weigh the metal.'

Galeran was struck by the man's zestful air. He looked through a door that opened onto the yard and gave a start when he saw Dame Mahaut sitting calmly in the shade of an apple tree.

'Go and say hello to my fiancée, Sir, while we talk business,' said the smith smugly. 'She owes you a great deal, and I do too!'

The young woman smiled at him. She wore a white dress such as widows sometimes wear, for white is the colour of resurrection. She amused herself by weaving a crown of ivy and daisies. Near her in a neglected vegetable garden strutted three white hens and a pretty black cock. Mahaut sensed Galeran's unease and gestured to him to come and sit next to her.

'You did not expect to find me here, Sir? Master Giffard said I should not stay at the inn on my own. You know, Giffard was one of my customers when I was working in a bawdy house in Saint-Gaudens.'

She gave the knight a provocative look. Galeran merely smiled in response.

'I know that, Dame Mahaut,' he said.

'No, knight, you know nothing,' said Mahaut, her eyes suddenly burning with anger. 'People like you know nothing!'

'You are right, Mahaut,' said Galeran softly. 'Enlighten me.'

After a long silence the young woman began to speak as though in a dream.

'You have seen my mother's house? It looks more like an animal's den with its earth walls and roof made of rushes. But I liked it. I ran barefoot by the river, among the wild birds. I caught frogs and hedgehogs to make soup with, I made whistles from willow branches. The children of the town mocked my wretchedness and threw stones at me. But I could always run faster than them! At the age of nine, knight, I was already a pretty little thing. My father, a noble like yourself, came to fetch me. He carried me off to his crumbling manor in a land where it was eternally cold and wet. You can imagine what he did with me when he got me there, and he did not stop until I was no longer a child, for then he feared the consequences!

'He brought me back to Chartres and my mother called me a whore and put me out of her house. A whore I am, and a whore I was, good Sir! So I took to the roads, I begged, I stole clothes from washhouses and eggs from hen-houses, I slept in haystacks. Then I met up with a hawker who told me the sun always shone in his region in the south. So I went with him on his mule, and I paid for the trip with the only currency I possessed. By the time we got to Saint-Gaudens I had got a bit of flesh back on my bones, and the hawker sold me to a whorehouse that had something of a reputation in the town.

'And that is where Jehan became my client. He loved me, and he sold all he had to buy me and take me back from whence I came. I wanted to have my revenge on all those who had spat on me. If I'd know it would be the death of Jehan . . . '

Mahaut's face fell into her hands.

'You know,' she said after a long silence, 'women like me cannot live without protection. I was lost when Jehan died. The goldsmith saw me at the ordeal and was smitten. He wants to marry me, but he'll have to go where I please. Jehan didn't leave me in need, you know, and I'll get a good price for the inn!'

Galeran looked at her and smiled.

'Thank you, Dame Mahaut, for confiding in me.'

'I don't know why I did!' she said, clenching her little fists. 'I do not like people of your sort . . . I mean . . . But I own I have a lot to thank you for. Malon told me what you did.'

'You owe me nothing, Mahaut. It is I who have learned from you. But tell me, why were you so harsh with La Doëtte?'

'So Ausanne told you about that,' said Mahaut with a vague smile. 'How do you think women like me survive if they don't fight tooth and nail for everything they have? Even if it sometimes means going over the top!'

'But beating a girl almost to death?'

'I do not expect you to understand,' replied Mahaut, shrugging her frail shoulders. 'But I have never been a servant, and I do not like them! They are all of the same breed, you have to watch them. They pretend to obey but deep down they mock you, they steal from you, they spy on you and they spread malicious gossip!'

'They're not all like that.'

'I tell you, I fear those girls, and La Doëtte was the worst of the lot with her frightened rabbit's eyes. If she had done nothing wrong then why was she so fearful?

'And,' she went on, her eyes glowing like two little lamps, 'you don't really think you can still have a soft heart if you have lived as I have for so many years? Thanks to Jehan I had become what I wanted to become, and I was enjoying it. But I was still uneasy, truth to tell. Everyone said I was a bastard, and doubtless my servants heard this. That's why I never kept them long. I knew they were jealous of me, and some of them were running after my man and that got my blood up. So I took it all out on Doëtte. I went too far and I'm ashamed of that. But I swear to you by Our Lady, after that I never even twisted her ear or pulled her hair again!'

Galeran could not help but smile.

'There is one thing I still do not understand, Dame Mahaut,' he said. 'Why did Ausanne hate you so? It cannot be due to La Doëtte alone.'

'I have often asked myself the same question, Sir. Ausanne was born, as they say, with a silver spoon in her mouth, and I think people like that harden their hearts and tell themselves they are superior to the rest of us. Even when I was a girl she despised me, and she and Jérôme and Nivelon were always pelting me with stones! You can see why her pious manners never impressed me. And her family was no longer so rich these last few years, so when she saw a hussy like me coming back home, rich and dressed like a princess, that can't have pleased her. And on top of that her father had to come and borrow money off Jehan!'

'I see,' said the knight as he stood up. 'I think I have got my answer.'

Mahaut had by now completed her ivy crown. She placed it over her brown hair and smiled a strange smile.

'Am I not pretty?' she asked.

'Like a nymph,' said Galeran gravely.

'What is a nymph?'

'You are a nymph, Mahaut!'

As Galeran and Giffard rode away from the goldsmith's, Mahaut stood at the door and watched the pair disappear into the distance.

The knight turned after a while and smiled at Giffard. The merchant returned his smile with a touch of philosophy.

'We find good in the most surprising of places, do we not, Sir?' he asked. 'And as our good Lord has told us, harlots and sinners shall enter before us into the Kingdom of Heaven.'

Que ceci soit la fin du livre mais non la fin de la recherche.

Bernard de Clairvaux

Author's note

The French art historian Émile Mâle wrote of the sculptures on the centre portal of Chartres cathedral:

'It was not only the sculptors of Saint-Denis who were called to work in Chartres in 1145. Master glaziers accompanied them, and their work is contemporaneous.

'The artist of the centre portal was one of the most important men at the cathedral of Chartres. There is a strange poetry in the smiling queens he created. It is the poetry of Breton lays, and will soon be the poetry of the Knights of the Round Table.'

Of the twelfth-century stained-glass window representing the Jesse tree, a window which survived several fires that caused great damage to the cathedral, Mâle wrote:

'The characters on the Jesse tree are depicted against a background of an almost supernatural blue. Neither the oriental sky nor the most precious of sapphires can rival this blue that stirs us like a revelation from another world.'

This blue is still visible in the cathedral of Notre Dame de Chartres, some eight hundred and fifty years later.

La Cuisine d'Hermine
Medieval recipes

The cuisine of the twelfth century made great use of spices and was much more exotic than modern cooking. At the time there were many common sayings that invoked spices, such as 'to find cinnamon in a phoenix's nest', and it was held that pepper trees were guarded by serpents which had to be burned in order to get black pepper.

In the Middle Ages spices were a very valuable commodity. It was said that in Europe the wind knocked dead branches off trees, but that in the Orient it blew down trees from Paradise, and these trees bore spices.

The more common spices at the time were: cloves, cinnamon, nutmeg, ginger, black pepper, cardamom, mace (made from the dried aril around the nutmeg seed), zedoary (a variety of curcuma), saffron. Galingale was less widely used due to its relative rarity.

Hippocras

A cordial drink made of wine flavoured with spices, very much in vogue in the Middle Ages. Often drunk after a meal or with oublies, wafer-thin cakes of pastry. Hermine likes to take a cup to aid digestion when she eats her *taillis aux épices*.

1 litre of good red wine
350g honey (or 350g sugar)
1 cinnamon stick
3 slices of fresh ginger
12 cloves
1 sprinkling of mace
nutmeg

galingale
1 rennet apple, sliced
1 dozen almonds, unpeeled

Grind the spices together. If using sugar, mix half of it with the spices. Take a deep pot and heat the wine and the honey (or the rest of the sugar). Slowly add the spices and mix. When the honey (or sugar) has melted and all the contents are well mixed, remove the pot from the heat.

Crush the almonds and place them along with the apple in a cloth filter. Pour in the wine. The hippocras should emerge clear and red. Bottle it and store in a cellar away from the light. Serve only to those seeking strong stimulation.

Potage à la Vierge (Our Lady's Soup)

One of Dame Hermine's favourite recipes.

1 litre stock
1 roast chicken breast
10cl crème fraîche
4 eggs
50g fresh breadcrumbs
12 fresh, peeled almonds
salt and pepper
150g stale bread crusts

Boil the eggs for nine minutes. Run them under cold water and peel. Discard the white.

Gently heat a quarter-litre of stock (having removed the fat that formed on top if it was left to go cold) along with the breadcrumbs. Bring to the boil and transfer to a vegetable mill with the chicken, the egg yolks and the almonds.

Add the cream, season to taste and place in a bain-marie (the sauce will turn if you put it directly over the heat).

Remove any remaining bread from the bread crusts. Cut the crusts into four-centimetre squares and place in an earthenware dish.

Pour the remaining stock and place in a moderately heated oven for fifteen minutes. Add the sauce, stir and serve immediately.

Lait Lardé

This should be made a day before serving.

250g lean, smoked bacon
1 litre milk
8 eggs
ginger
saffron
lard
salt and pepper

Remove the rind from the bacon and cut the meat into small squares.

Grease a pan with the rind and cook the bacon over a low heat until it is brown.

Bring the milk to the boil.

Break the eggs into a bowl. Season with a pinch of saffron and a pinch of ginger as you beat the eggs with a wooden spoon. Gradually pour in the milk and add the bacon.

Pour into a soufflé dish and place in a bain-marie. Cook in a moderate oven for thirty-five minutes.

Let the dish go cold. Cover and leave overnight.

Remove from the dish, cut into thin slices and fry in lard. Season to taste.

Serve very hot.

Oeufs Rotis à la Broche

8 large eggs
1 bunch each of parsley, marjoram, sage and mint
40g butter
8 thyme leaves

1 pinch ginger
1 pinch saffron
salt and pepper

Use brown eggs with a solid shell. With a pin make a small hole in each egg through which a skewer can be passed. Hold the eggs vertically and blow into the holes to pour their insides onto a dish. Put the shells aside for later use.

. Chop the herbs very finely and mix them in as you beat the eggs. Fry in butter until the mix resembles a runny omelette. Add the ginger, saffron, thyme and salt and pepper.

Chop up, make eight equal parts and fill each egg shell. Gently insert the skewer into the stuffed eggs.

Turn over a low flame for five minutes. Serve on the skewer.

Galimafrée

600g leg of lamb leftovers
300g onions
80g butter
2 soup spoons verjuice or vinegar
1 pinch of ginger
salt and pepper
fried croûtons

Dice the lamb leftovers.

Peel the onions and chop finely. Braise the onions in the butter, the verjuice (or vinegar) and the ginger. Add salt and pepper. Cover the pan and leave over a low heat for thirty minutes.

Add the lamb. Cook for another fifteen minutes.

Sprinkle the croûtons over the top and serve very hot.

Sauce Cameline

Slice some bread and toast lightly. Heat red wine, vinegar, cinnamon, pepper and ginger in a pot over a low heat and add the toast.

Leave to cool and strain. This sauce will stay good for up to a week if it is kept in pots. It can be used for roast meat.

Sauce de Trahison

Make a stock of red wine and vinegar. Add a cinnamon stick and leave overnight. Chop some onion and some bacon and fry. Place this in a dish with toast dipped in the stock. Add some mustard and a good dose of honey. The result is something of a shock for our modern taste buds!

Oublies

From the Latin *oblata*, meaning something offered. Oublies, also called obleys, were sold in the street.

250g honey
250g flour
2 eggs
30g butter

You will need a waffle iron for this recipe.

Mix ten centilitres of cold water with the honey. Put the flour in a dish. Make a hollow in the middle of the flour, add the eggs, mix and gradually add in the honey.

Melt half the butter and mix it with the flour. The pastry should be thick enough to be rolled.

Make around thirty little balls. Heat the waffle iron until very hot, grease with butter, insert the pastry balls, close tightly and leave for forty-five seconds. Regrease the waffle iron after every five oublies.

Serve hot or cold.

Taillis aux Épices

This light dessert is Hermine's favourite. The almond milk base needs to be prepared the day before.

120g almonds, unpeeled
150g fresh breadcrumbs
150g currants
2 apples, diced
4 spoonfuls honey
1 pinch cinnamon
1 pinch ginger
1 pinch saffron

Soak the almonds in still mineral water and put the currants in a bowl along with a drop of eau de vie. Leave overnight.

Peel the almonds (Hermine does this by putting them in boiling water, draining them and running them under cold water. The brown skin then simply falls off when touched). Place them in a litre of still mineral water in a copper pot.

Add the breadcrumbs, honey and diced apple and heat gently until the mixture begins to thicken. Then add the currants, cinnamon, ginger and saffron, and the mixture should turn a nice golden yellow colour. Place this sweet-smelling dough in a cake tin on greaseproof paper. Leave to cool for several hours.

This *taillis* is served chilled. Cut it into slices and wash down with a warm drink such as hippocras.

A Medieval Lexicon

Autricum: the name the Romans gave Chartres during their rule over Gaul.

Breeches: a garment covering the loins and thighs.

Carnutes: Chartres was named after the Carnutes, a Celtic tribe who made it their principal Druidic centre.

Chausses: a tight-fitting garment covering the feet and legs, usually made of chain mail.

Cistercian: a monastic order founded in 1098 and named after the original establishment at Cîteaux (Latin: Cistercium), a locality in Burgundy, near Dijon. It expanded rapidly under Saint Bernard de Clairvaux and by his death in 1153 had 338 abbeys across Europe and the Mediterranean.

Compline: the last of the seven canonical hours of the divine office.

Consoude: a herb to which healing virtues were attributed.

Dubbing: the ceremony by which a man is made a knight by the ritual of tapping on his shoulder with a sword.

Goliard: one of a number of wandering scholars in twelfth- and thirteenth-century Europe famed for their riotous behaviour, intemperance and composition of satirical and ribald Latin verse.

Hippocras: a cordial drink made of wine flavoured with spices.

Jesse tree: a geneaological tree representing the genealogy of Christ, from the root of Jesse (the father of King David), used in churches in the Middle Ages as a decoration for a wall, window, vestment or in the form of a large-branched candlestick.

Matins: the first of the seven canonical hours of prayer.

Montjoy: commemorative pile of stone laid by pilgrims in which they placed crosses or statues of the Virgin or the saints.

Oblate: a person dedicated to a monastic or religious life.

Oublie: a thin cake of pastry, or wafer. Also called obley.
Prévôté: the place where the Provost, a local magistrate and bailiff, has his offices and where his men are garrisoned.
Prime: the second of the seven canonical hours of the divine office, at sunrise.
Quolibet: from the Latin 'Quod libet' – any question in philosophy or theology proposed as an exercise in argument or disputation.
Seven liberal arts: consisting of the trivium – grammar, rhetoric and logic – and the quadrivium – arithmetic, geometry, astronomy, and music.
Sext: the fourth of the seven canonical hours of the divine office. Originally the sixth hour of the day (noon).
Vespers: evening prayers or devotions.

Historical figures of the twelfth century

Pierre Abélard (1079–1142): Scholastic philosopher and theologian. He is also known for his poetry and for his celebrated love affair with Héloïse.

Aliénor (Eleanor) of Acquitaine (1122–1204): perhaps the most powerful woman in twelfth-century Europe. Queen of France (1137–52) by her marriage to Louis VII and Queen of England (1154–89) by her marriage to Henry II. Mother of the English Kings Richard I and John.

Bernard de Clairvaux (1091–1153): Cistercian monk and mystic, the founder and abbot of the abbey of Clairvaux and one of the most influential churchmen of his time.

Louis VII (1120–80): Capetian King of France who pursued a long rivalry, marked by recurrent warfare and continuous intrigue, with Henry II of England. Also called Louis le Jeune.

Suger (1081–1151): abbot and adviser to Kings Louis VI and VII, whose supervsion of the rebuilding of the abbey church of Saint-Denis was instrumental in the development of the Gothic style of architecture. Acted as regent in 1147–49 while Louis VII was away on the Second Crusade.

Thibaud (Theobald) IV (1093–1152): Count of Blois and of Chartres.

Geoffroy de Lèves: Bishop of Chartres at the time of this novel and a friend of Abbé Suger.